THE UPPERTHONG THUNDERBOLT

AND OTHER STORIES

John Simes

With Chris Simes, Vanessa J. Chapman
and Gary Maguire

Collingwood Publishing & Media Ltd

JOHN SIMES

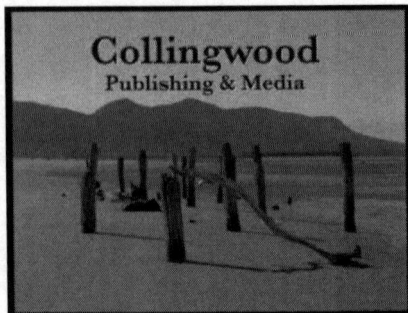

Collingwood
Publishing & Media

ISBN: 978-1-9996359-3-0

Books by John Simes

The Dream Factory Quadrilogy:

The Dream Factory (2017), Matador
A Game of Chess (2018), Collingwood
Who Is This Little Witch? (2022), Collingwood
Cape Farewell (2022), Collingwood

Short stories

The Upperthong Thunderbolt (2021), Collingwood

Education books

Network 1, Network 2, Beginnings,

JOHN SIMES

For Leo, Rosie, Max, Charlie, Billy and Ben – thanks for all the joys you bring us.

CONTENTS

ACKNOWLEDGMENTS

I owe an immense debt once again to a terrific reading team, including Jo Simes, Vanessa Chapman, John Gardner, Chris Simes, Nick Johns, Louise Payne, Jo Thomson, Felicity Dunworth, Louise Wainwright, Gary Maguire, Lucy Atkinson, Cherie Woolmer, Rebecca Wynter, Kate Morley, and many more. Thanks also to Phil Johns (PJStudios) www.werespond.uk for design and website development, Joni Hawkes for expert book launch guidance, and Jill Gubbins for event planning. I am particularly grateful to the wonderfully gifted recording artist Emma Tricca for allowing this humble scribbler to use her lyrics and title in the story *Julian's Wings*. I am thrilled that many of these tales will be appearing in online publications including *Storgy Magazine*; *Om* and *Stoggies Farm* have appeared in *The Menteur* – the magazine of the Paris School of Arts and Culture.

I must also thank the inspirational and supportive Modbury Creative Writing Group: Mary McClarey, Nancy Owen, Meg Foster, John Curry, Lucy Brown, Mavis Pilbeam, Ron Wood, Belinda Chesman, led by Peter Hitchen.

Finally, gratitude to my brilliant editor, Angela Brown, and superb copyeditor Maddie York.

Profits from the sales of this book will be donated to the fantastic charity Refuge www.refuge.org.uk whose work to protect women and children experiencing domestic abuse has never been more urgently needed.

FOREWORD

This potpourri of stories is inspired by all the amazing people I have known and taught. I love writing comedy, stories about the supernatural and ghosts, stories about important life issues, thrillers, romances; tales about our progress as we walk the jagged pathway of living through these turbulent times.

Readers of *The Dream Factory* and *A Game of Chess* will recognise some of the characters – Reverend Thomas, Miss B, Yvonne and, of course, Peter and Navinda, and the village of Ringmore (aka Dingwell!). I am fascinated by the transformational power of human love, our need to believe in something outside of ourselves, and our desire to be something more remarkable than we can be – perhaps? In these stories, you will find your many selves. Enjoy the whole crazy ride.

John Simes

THE UPPERTHONG THUNDERBOLT

**A naïve young vicar plays snooker with the locals in an
old Yorkshire village....**

T he door opened. Widow Wendy smiled coyly. "Well,
hello, boys."

"Hello, Ma," said Nobby.

Wendy drew on her Capstan full strength, before
expelling a plume of blue smoke in Nobby's direction. "I
weren't talking to thee, Norbert Thrustle. Nor that fleabag,
Gilbert Entwistle. I were talkin' to 'andsome boy."

"Reckon she means you, Reverend," said Nobby,
resignedly.

Smiling weakly, I looked at Nobby – thin and wiry in his
faded tweed suit, his soft grey eyes blinking beneath his tweed
trilby. Gilbert, the village shopkeeper, was more amply
proportioned, with cherry-red cheeks and untidy eyebrows
under his baker boy cap. I struggled out of my waterproofs,
curious to find out the real reason the glamorously antique
Widow Wendy had invited a cluster of wrinkly pensioners to
her home each week.

It was a stormy Wednesday evening across the windswept
Pennine hills. Lightning flickered white on the distant peaks,
and thunder boomed through the valleys. But it was snooker
night at Widow Wendy's, and she enjoyed holding court in her

kitchen. From a high stool at the breakfast bar, she queened over the little group of ragtag locals who had stumbled through the dark of Upperthong village to her door. Presently, we would descend like condemned souls into the gothic subterranean snooker room in the cellar of Shufflebottom House, Wendy's graceful and ornate Victorian villa.

The house also lorded over the tumbled miners' cottages and cobbled lanes of Upperthong, where children queued for the school bus with their portly mothers and, on winter evenings, the warm glow of lamp and log fire charmed the locals to the hearth of the Royal Oak pub. To be invited to play snooker at Widow Wendy's was meant to be an honour – but frequent visits to the village by the Grim Reaper had dwindled the numbers of cue-toting old buffers, who had become increasingly fearful of an imminent departure to the afterlife. I wondered whether extending the invitation to the new local vicar was to provide a little divine insurance.

"You want to be careful, Reverend." My housekeeper, Mrs Skillet, had pulled a face when I'd told her where I was going. "You want to be careful, Reverend." She stood in her blue housecoat and new pixie-bob hairdo, and cradling a feather duster like a posy, she had cast a critical eye as I stood self-consciously in my best jeans and burgundy clerical shirt.

"Oh, do brush your hair, Reverend, while you still got some! You look a bit young and innocent for that woman."

Wrinkling her nose, she adjusted my collar and brushed fluff from my shirt. "*That* Widow Wendy! And all *those* men!"

I smiled. "Are they in need of some spiritual guidance, Mrs Skillet?"

She stared at me though her pink-rimmed spectacles. "I should say so. Just watch yourself with those folks, Reverend. Queer as a bottle o' chips."

I was getting used to her broad Yorkshire accent. As a baby, I was adopted by a family in Penistone and acquired their softer West Riding tones before being sent to boarding school. "They'll teach you to speak proper!" said my mother.

During my first ministry in Upperthong, my middle-class accent had induced stares from some locals. "That reverend must think we're all pit ponies," said one old man in the village shop.

But I was here now. In the slightly unnerving presence of the queen of Upperthong. "Good evening, erm, widow … Widow Wendy …" I stammered. Nobby hung his trilby on a coat peg while Gilbert struggled out of his overcoat. Widow Wendy looked at me intently.

"You 'aven't seen me in church, 'ave you vicar?" she said, mischievously. She fluttered her eyelashes beneath her bleached beehive. "You see, folks say I'm a bit of a naughty girl, but you might just 'ave somethin' I want."

"Oh … erm …" I had a lump the size of a billiard ball in my throat. "What could I have that you would want, Widow Wen–?"

"Wendy is the name, Reverend. Plain, simple Wendy. And what be yours?"

Wendy managed to keep her eyes firmly fixed on me while topping up her sherry glass. I noticed the bottle was nearly empty and she wavered slightly.

"Thomas," I blurted. "No, Tom. Reverend Tom."

Wendy's eyebrows elevated. "Reverend Thomas!"

"Just Tom. Plain Tom," I said, recovering some composure.

"I see you've brought your own cue. Looks like a right beauty." Her eyes swept to the buffalo-leather cue case. I placed it on the breakfast bar and flipped the gold clasp. The lid tipped back to reveal an antique Furkiss and Ferret snooker cue. Soft gasps of awe and reverence issued from the open-mouthed ancients, and the air filled with energy and excitement. Aged fingers extended to touch the slender dart of finest Canadian maple, hand-spliced with coal-black lignum vitae; it was graced by an endcap of gold and engraved with an image of a ferret.

"I assume the Reverend Slaughterhouse owned it," I said. "I found it in his study." In that moment, I realised how much make-up Wendy was wearing. Her cherry red lips and heavily blushed cheeks were battling gamely with the track lines of old age.

"That's a very special cue, that is," said Nobby. "Make sure you looks after it, Reverend Tom." He winked at Wendy.

"Antique," I reckon," said Wendy. "Champion, that!"

"Wendy'll chalk it for thee if you like," sniggered Gilbert.

"You keep a civil tongue in yer 'ead, young Gilbert," barked Wendy. The cherry red lips had now become a thin red line. "One sniff of a barmaid's apron and you're dancing a jig!"

Gilbert bridled. "Chance would be a fine thing," he sniffed. "Are we allowed to 'ave a beer, Wendy, or must we all die of thirst?"

Wendy reached for a large tin mug and placed it on the bar. "Put some gold in me pot, boys!" We reached into our pockets and tumbled loose change into the mug.

"Old Stan used to keep his false teeth in that mug," said Nobby.

"And his glass eye," said Gilbert, pulling three bottles of Methuselah's Old Wrinkly from the fridge.

"Wendy 'ad that eye made into a door knocker when 'e snuffed it!" said Nobby, with a wink. "She always wanted 'im to keep an eye on the place when she was out!"

"Stop your nonsense, Norbert Thrustle. You'll frighten off our new recruit. It's a pleasure to see you, Reverend Tom. Some folks forget that I'm still a woman, Reverend. Same wishes, same desires, same … needs." Wendy smiled sweetly, but her missing premolar added a soupçon of menace. "I see you noticed my missin' pearly, Reverend Tom. Reckon my poor dead 'usband knew somethin' about that!"

"Stan didn't nick your nibbler, Wendy," said Nobby.

"Pure gold, it were!" protested Wendy.

Gilbert bristled. "What would Stan 'ave done with it, Wendy? Go down the pub and swap it for a pint?"

"Put it on a horse, more like," murmured Nobby, who picked up his beer. "Come on, Reverend. Me and Gilbert will show thee 'ow to play the great game."

We grabbed our beers and descended the wooden stairs as a cork popped in the kitchen; Wendy had dug out another bottle of Bristol Cream. "Poor old Wendy. She 'ates missing a spoke," said Gilbert. "Don't look good on an old bike!"

"Penny farthing, more like," said Nobby. "Not easy if you're one meat-chisel light of a full set."

"When I lost me pickle stabbers," said Gilbert, "I couldn't eat a gherkin. Then I 'ad to 'ave all me teeth out." Gilbert's weathered hand reached into his mouth and extracted his false teeth. Taking them between finger and thumb, he clicked them together as if in conversation. "Wendy wouldn't kiss me no more," grumbled the dentures.

Nobby collapsed into a wheezy laugh while Gilbert gurned grotesquely, his lips rolling inwards, as if about to consume his chin. I winced.

"You mean you and Wendy were ..." I hesitated.

"In a manner of speaking, yes, Reverend," chattered the teeth.

Nobby guffawed as Gilbert reinstalled his dentures. "She's a wonderful woman," said Nobby. "Don't underestimate 'er, Reverend."

"No, don't do that Reverend." Gilbert stared intently at me. "Wendy always gets what she wants, Reverend. *Always*." He raised a warning finger before his wrinkled lips broke into a grin. "C'mon, Reverend Tom. As the Angel Gabriel said, 'If we fail at love, there's always the green baize!'"

Nobby opened the cellar door and tugged the light pull. I caught my breath when I saw what was inside. The mahogany snooker table stood like a majestic ship of state in its harbour of plush crimson drapes, sleek woollen carpet, and picture frames of eucalyptus.

A relic of the Indian Raj, its hand-carved oak legs as stout as an elephant's, the table had witnessed the rise and fall of the British Empire but remained loyal to the dream of imperial invincibility and faraway lands. Its green baize shone a luminous emerald – as dazzling as the mint juleps, gin slings and Chartreuse liqueurs that I imagined were consumed by bedecked army officers and their fragrant wives.

A matrix of coolie shades flooded the table with light, dancing over the coloured balls. Serried ranks of snooker cues stood in racks, as lances lined up ready for combat. Photographs of the great and good from Upperthong adorned the walls which were lined with the sumptuous maroons and indigoes of vintage William Morris wallpapers. A walnut scoreboard, its brass sliders glittering, stood on its wooden stand, also ready for battle. A gothic arched window looked over the immaculate lawns, blazed white by the storm as thunder boomed once again across the village.

Gilbert drew the red curtains across. "We can do without that clatter!"

Donning pure white cotton gloves, Nobby gathered the snooker balls into the wooden triangle. He squatted down, expertly manoeuvring the rack into position. Next, he placed black, pink, blue, brown, green, and yellow balls precisely on their spots. With a sigh of pleasure, he plucked the white cue ball from his pocket and polished it lovingly in his gloved hands before placing it on the green baize.

Another rattle of thunder rumbled across the village. Gilbert grunted and pulled the drapes firmly closed. "Fancy the Almighty be shiftin' 'is commode, Reverend. P'raps 'e fancies rearranging things a bit?" Gilbert hurled his coat and cap on to a chaise longue and placed his wire spectacles on his chubby nose.

I hung my raincoat on a hook and set my beer down on a ledge. Once again, I opened the leather case, and lifted out the cue, the polished maple spear reflecting the light from a

Dragonfly standard lamp. "You'll need this, Reverend!" Nobby said, handing me a cube of blue chalk.

Gilbert unsheathed his cue from its plastic case and glanced enviously as I chalked the end of mine. "Fancy we'll not stand much chance tonight, Norbert. Not with the Reverend toting a Furkiss & Ferret and wi' God on his side!" Another peel of thunder rolled across Upperthong and the lights flickered. "Eee, see what I mean!"

"Eh up, Reverend Tom," said Nobby. "As special guest, you takes first go."

"I'll not be very good, I fear." I settled into position, extending my left hand on to the baize, the cue sliding into the V of forefinger and thumb. "Last time I did this was at the student union bar at college."

I squinted along the cue, directing the tip towards the base of the white ball. The cue felt incredibly natural and fit snugly. A soft click, and the white ball raced towards the red pack; it glanced off the final red, before speeding for the rear cushion. I watched as it rebounded off the side and came rolling back towards me. I lifted my hand from the table, and the ball kissed the cushion beneath me and revolved softly to a perfect position behind the brown ball. Gilbert gasped.

"By 'eck, Reverend, that were champion!" said Nobby. "Bloody snooker, first pop!"

"Or dead jammy," huffed Gilbert.

"Just a stroke of luck, lads," I said.

"Eh up, don't get a monk on, Gilbert."

I stepped aside as Gilbert moved to the end of the table. "You'll be as 'appy as a pig in muck after that, Reverend." He bent down and farted perfunctorily.

"'Ere, who guffed?" said Nobby. "Reeks like a dung 'eap!"

"Archangel Gabriel," said Gilbert, as he sent the cue ball bouncing off two cushions before it clattered into the pink.

"Foul!" shouted Nobby. "That's six penn'orth to Reverend Tom." He slid the brass slider on the scoreboard.

"Eee, look, you've broken up the pack, Gilbert. Reverend Tom can clean up!"

I walked to the side of the table. A red was invitingly poised for the rear pocket. Bending down, I extended my arm once again. The red bounded into the pocket and the cue ball stunned perfectly for the black. I paced to the other side and leaned on to the table. The maple dart stabbed, and the black ball skittered across the baize and plunged into the pocket. Gilbert groaned and collapsed morosely into a chair.

"'Tis all up for thee this frame, I reckon," said Nobby.

"Great shot, Reverend," said Gilbert. "Don't forget your beer."

"In a tick," I said. I was enjoying myself. The cue felt beautifully balanced and weighted, and I was playing with a sublime grace and touch that was positively supernatural if not divine. Red. *Bang*. Black. *Bang*. Another four reds and blacks tumbled into the pockets, as Gilbert dug his hands into his own, and slouched farther in his seat. Finally, my luck ran out as the pink shunned the middle pocket.

"Eee, look, 'e missed one," said Nobby. "Fifty-six!" he announced triumphantly and moved the brass slider. More thunder, sending the lights flickering again. "Oh, ah. Reckon the lights 'ave gone out on thy chances, Gilbert. Bet thou't need snookers."

"I'm nae done yet, Norbert. Thankee," muttered Gilbert. He wandered resignedly back to the table and bent over the baize, his tweed trousers expanding to contain his ample rear. He inhaled deeply as his paunch threatened to smother the pink.

I supped my beer. It tasted very bitter and I held the glass up to the light.

"Deh, bugger!" Gilbert groaned as the cue ball sped towards the blue before careering into the rear pocket.

"Foul!" cried Nobby. "That's another four points, Reverend Tom!"

Nobby's voice seemed to have come from a distant place, and the room suddenly appeared to be floating. I was feeling extremely strange. I dropped my beer glass and collapsed into a rack of snooker cues before tumbling into a chair. My head lolled, and my eyes wanted to close. I must have been gaping like a codfish. Another thunderclap rattled over the house, and the room lights dimmed before they blacked out completely. A door opened. A shaft of white light blazed down the stairwell and illuminated Wendy, who stood as motionless as a ghost in the doorway. The coolie lamps flickered briefly.

"'Ow's it going, Reverend Tom?" asked Wendy, the flashing lights adding to the drama of her appearance. "You see, I always gets what I want, Reverend Tom. Always."

I saw her face, gaunt and white as the moon, before I passed out.

* * *

"There's someone to see you, Reverend."

I peered over the edge of the duvet. Mrs Skillet was looking down at me, blinking through her spectacles. What time was it? Where was I?

"What happened?" I asked. "What day is it, Mrs S?"

"It's Friday afternoon, Reverend. You've been asleep for thirty-six hours."

I struggled to comprehend. "You mean, you mean …"

"Constable Drudge is here," she said severely.

"The police? What …? Why?" I blathered.

"I did warn you, Reverend. Going to see that woman would come to no good."

Painfully, I sat up in bed, struggling to remember. My memory had gone blank. "What on earth happened?"

Mrs Skillet looked at me pityingly. "You should have taken my advice. It's four o'clock in the afternoon. Now the police are here. PC Drudge is waiting downstairs."

"Alright, alright! I'll get dressed."

"You can do that on your own, I think, Reverend," said Mrs Skillet primly. "Seen all I wish to see." She left the room.

I swung my legs out of the bed and tried to stand, but the room lurched, and I staggered into the dressing table. The creature that stared from the mirror was no longer the slender, sparkling-eyed young curate of Upperthong, but a haggard barbarian with tousled hair and wild staring eyes. Indeed, I was sporting a tremendous shiner. I looked as though I had done ten rounds of bare-knuckle fist-fighting – and lost.

I wove off to the bathroom and stood in the shower, still wearing my bed socks. I let the water drum therapeutically on my crown before tipping the contents of a shampoo bottle over my head. I clumsily lathered and rinsed my body before reaching for the towel. I stepped out, hurled my sodden bed socks back into the shower and slithered back to the bedroom. Averting my eyes from the mirror, I hunted for some clothes. A few minutes later, I presented myself in the drawing room.

Constable Titus Drudge sat on a dining chair by the mantelpiece, where he had placed a mug of tea - and his police helmet, its silver badge lovingly polished. His dark-blue police uniform, and glittering buttons were at odds with his bullish features, bloodshot cheeks and morose eyebrows. There were many versions of this face in the village. This was a man, I quickly decided, whose forlorn expression could dishearten an optimist from fifty paces. I imagined the sunflowers in my garden wilting under his gaze. He looked up briefly as I entered and pulled a black notebook from his top pocket.

"Now, then, Reverend, tha's bin in a reet pickle!"

I gaped as Mrs Skillet entered with a plate of chocolate biscuits. "There you are Titus. Your favourites."

"Aye, Thelma. Long time since brickfust!" He nibbled a Hobnob before turning to me once more. "Now. What's tha' doin' art Widow Wendy's, Toe-mass?"

"Snooker! I … I went to play snooker."

"Snooker, tha' says. Snooker! So wha' wus tha' doin' snoggin' the Archangel Gabriel i' the muddle o' the neet?"

A wave of horror flowed over me. "I was what?!"

"Thomas," said Mrs Skillet. "I heard a noise in the garden, and I came out to find you slumped on the statue with your arms around its neck. You were talking to it."

"Oh, my sainted aunt! No, I can't have!"

"Thou did just thart! Made a bloody row. Someone called the police. And me and Thelma got thee back in the house."

"So, so how did I get back from Widow Wendy's house?"

"Those men dragged you back and left you in the garden."

"Nobby and Gilbert?"

"I wouldn't be calling them *men* myself," said Mrs Skillet.

PC Drudge snorted. "Tha's lucky thou weren't left naked as a new-born bairn."

"They did that to the last traffic warden," said Mrs. Skillet.

"Aye, 'e was found in 't graveyard, sittin' on statue of a pit pony, just wearing 'is cap!" chortled the constable. "They got 'im cos 'e nicked old Stan for leaving his trailer of horse manure outside the W.I. Now we can park wherever we like." Mrs Skillet tried to suppress a smile.

PC Drudge drained the last of his tea and sighed. "Let me give thee some advice, Reverend. Thong folk don't like change. Doesn't pay to go causin' a stir. Know what I mean?"

"Cause a stir? I've only been here for a week!"

"Bottom line is, Reverend, thou wert as blotto as a budgerigar in a belfry. Thou shoulda known better!"

"But I wasn't drunk. I had one beer. What in the world happened?"

Mrs Skillet stood up and walked slowly to the fireplace. She gave me a sympathetic smile. "Perhaps they slipped him one, Titus."

"Aye." PC Drudge grinned. "P'raps thou 'ad a Mickey Finn."

"A what?"

"You heard of a Penistone Pistol? A Slaithwaite Slammer? Round 'ere, they call it a Thong Thunderbolt." The policeman was now smiling broadly.

"A what? What the heck is in a Thong Thunderbolt?"

"It's an old recipe," Mrs Skillet murmured.

"Aye, that it is. Raw alcohol, snuff and gin." said the policeman gleefully. "Old Stan gave one to 'is horse when it were sick. It slept for a week. It were fine after that!"

"But I've been poisoned. You're the police! Aren't you going to arrest them?"

"Can't prove nothin'," sniffed PC Drudge. "We'll chat about it at the Lodge. I'll warn them not to do it again."

"Is that all?

"Be a bit more careful next time, Reverend. Remember, we lived 'ere all our lives. Thou's a newcomer. So, haul thy head in." He rose to his feet and took his helmet from the mantlepiece. "I'll see meself out, Thelma."

Mrs Skillet and I watched as the door closed. She turned towards me. "I did warn you, Thomas. But I never imagined they would do that to you."

"Folks don't like change. That's what PC Drudge said." I heaved a sigh.

"But they wouldn't have done it just because you were new. There must have been another reason." She looked intently at me through her spectacles.

I gestured helplessly. "I really have no idea, Mrs S. Perhaps I'm not the right vicar for Upperthong?"

"Listen, Reverend. When I found you in the garden, you didn't have your snooker cue." She was still looking at me keenly.

"I must have lost it."

"No, Reverend. Someone placed it outside the front door this morning. That used to be Stan's cue. He sold it to the Reverend Slaughterhouse to pay off his gambling debts."

I puffed out my cheeks. "The plot thickens, Mrs. S."

* * *

"We're really sorry, Reverend," said Gilbert.

"Yes, yes. We're really sorry," said Nobby.

PC Drudge inhaled. "They really are very, very sorry, Reverend," he pronounced solemnly. "And they've promised they won't do it again. Haven't you, gentlemen?"

"Aye, yes, we've promised, haven't we, Gilbert?"

Gilbert sniffed. "Aye. It won't 'appen again."

Nobby shook his head vigorously. "Nay, never 'appen again." His eyes flickered nervously beneath his tweed trilby. Gilbert shuffled uncomfortably in his seat and stared at his gnarled fingers.

"Never."

"Never."

I looked at them, sitting on the bench in the snug bar of the Royal Oak, looking for all the world like stuffed toys from a car-boot sale. But they were part of my flock and I was their shepherd. I felt like shooting them.

I had managed to perform the Sunday morning communion, albeit with a minor tremor or two. There were sheepish expressions from some of the congregation. Widow Wendy had made a dramatic appearance smiling beatifically from behind a black widow's veil which complemented a black lace mini dress with long bell sleeves, a low V-neckline and lettuce ruffle hems. Gilbert and Nobby had sat on either side, like elderly Labradors.

Wendy beamed at me relentlessly during my sermon, and kissed my cheek as she left, a gold tooth glinting in the spring morning sun. "See. I got what I wanted, eh, Reverend Tom," she whispered fragrantly, pressing a carefully folded note into my hand before stepping into a vintage Bugatti Coupe. "Please meet in the snug at Royal Oak, X," it said in elegant italics on cerise notepaper.

In the snug, I broke the silence. "I see Wendy rediscovered her golden pearly," I said, enjoying the vernacular. Gilbert and Nobby lowered their gazes once more. "Pray, how did that happen?" I enquired sweetly.

PC Drudge uncrossed his legs and placed his hands on his knees. "It were like this Reverend. It seems that one night, old Wendy were three sheets to the wind, and she told Stan he couldn't have any more brass to pay off his debts. So, when she were purring asleep, 'e nicked her spoke from a glass o' Steradent, and then hid it."

"Aye, said Nobby. "Stan told us on 'is deathbed."

"Did he say where he'd hidden it?" I said.

"Wi' his dying breath, old Stan said, 'Wendy's nipper's in the ferret!' said Nobby.

"In the ferret! *In* the ferret? What ferret?"

"Aye," muttered Gilbert. "We wondered that. So we hunted about Wendy's 'ouse for a stuffed ferret. Course we found one in't khazi, but it weren't in there."

"Went through all the antique shops. Woman at the W.I.'s bring and buy sale hit me with a bedpan cos she said I were givin' 'er stuffed ferret a funny look." said Nobby. "Called me a pervy twonk!"

"I'm not surprised," I said, finding this increasingly surreal. "So where did you find it?"

Gilbert took a deep breath. "It were in't snooker cue!"

"What my snooker cue?"

"Aye. The Furkiss and Ferret. We didn't know Stan had flogged it to the vicar. Wendy's spoke were felted in't chamber beneath the endcap. When thou was snoring, we unscrewed it and there it were!"

"Why didn't you just ask me?"

"We was scared o' Wendy," said Nobby. "When she saw it, she said, 'I want that, boys. Give Reverend the Upperthong Thunderbolt.' She allus kept a bottle of it in the fridge."

"Next to the tonic water," said Gilbert.

"Aye. Reverend Slaughterhouse made a mistake and poured it in his gin. 'E were out like a light."

Gilbert grunted. "We knew if we didn't, she'd chuck us out."

"Chuck you out?"

Nobby nodded. "Aye. She's our landlady. She lets us live in a cottage each in't village. But we 'ave to do what she says."

"Like I said, Reverend, Wendy allus gets what she wants."

There was a silence. I sat back in my chair and looked at the tobacco-coloured walls and the ceiling fan whirling slowly. My parishioners were all next door in the saloon bar. Through the glazed screen, I saw them nodding like hens, wearing their Sunday best, and the cackle of conversation and laughter seemed to float like confused music above our heads. But I had a decision to make. Was I, could I, be a part of this music? My first duty, I knew, was to forgive. It would be hard, but I knew I could do that. There was no other way. But could I nurture this wayward, raggedy flock? Protect the young, comfort the old, and bring light to a modern world that was lapping, like a ravenous ocean, at these peaceful Pennine shores?

"There's one more thing, vicar." Nobby leaned forward and solemnly removed his little trilby hat. I had decided that, despite everything, I liked Nobby. His trusting soft grey eyes were like my own, Mrs Skillet had said.

"Yes? What is it, Norbert?" I said, gently.

Nobby clasped his hands. "Thelma says you're a right fine man, Reverend. Other folks think so too." His hands were perspiring, I noticed, and a bead of sweat ran down his forehead. "She's afraid you're going to leave. But Thelma wants you to stay."

"Aye," said Gilbert.

"Aye," said PC Drudge.

I was suddenly very moved. Nobby's voice was pleasantly soft and caring. His hands wrung once more. "Nay, Thomas. There's more." He looked at Gilbert, who averted his eyes. A sudden silence had fallen on the saloon bar. Faces were pressed to the screen. Nobby was staring at me. A tear tumbled down his cheek.

"Shall I say this for thee, Norbert?" said PC Drudge. He patted Nobby's shoulder.

"Aye, please," sniffed Nobby.

"Thou wert raised in Penistone, I hear, Reverend," the policeman's eyebrows enquired.

"Yes, aye!" I blurted.

"A few year back, our Nobby here and Thelma ..." He hesitated.

"Yes," I said, suddenly feeling rather warm.

"They was younger then. And in love, see? Nobby and Thelma had a wee bairn. A baby," said the policeman, as if I hadn't understood the word.

Nobby suddenly burst out. "Little Reggie!" he sobbed. "Our little Reggie!" he cried. "But me and Thelma 'ad no money. No proper home."

"The bairn was given to a lady in Penistone. She adopted 'im," said PC Drudge.

"A right posh lass," said Gilbert. "She would write to Thelma, saying what a great lad thou was."

"It broke our hearts," said Nobby.

"She told us you'd become a poncey fashion designer then started vicarin'," said Gilbert.

But Nobby's grey eyes were now bloodshot with tears. He stared up at me with those grey eyes. *They were my eyes*!

"Excuse me! I need a moment!" I said and stood up.

"Aye, you go to bog, lad!" said Gilbert.

As I pushed open the door, I cast a backward glance. Gilbert and Nobby were in one another's arms, blubbering like infants. I strode into the toilet, stood in front of the washbasin, and stared into the cracked mirror. Nobby's grey eyes stared back at me, and there was something of Mrs Skillet's mouth about me. I trembled.

So, it was true. I was Reggie. Not Thomas. But I liked being Thomas. I was *doubting* Thomas. *Dutiful* Thomas.

Faithful Thomas. *Radical* Thomas. *Honest* Thomas. Thomas *the Reverend*. Not Reggie! The name evoked the image of a seedy bookmaker or used-car dealer, pockets stuffed with rolls of fifty-pound notes. Reggie, the minor gangster. The mob leader's dim accomplice. The driver of the getaway car. The dodgy repairman. The bald night club bouncer. The follicly challenged part-owner of a seedy strip club.

I snorted. What *Reggie* had ever changed the world for the better? What *Reggie* was revered, given a knighthood, honoured with a statue? Was there ever a Saint *Reggie*? Would King Henry II have even bothered to murder his errant archbishop, Thomas à Becket, if he had been called Reggie? Would Henry VIII's sinister interrogator have carried the same level of menace if he had been *Reggie* Cromwell? Unthinkable! Reverend Blooming Reggie!

I felt robbed, cheated of my identity. I had been abused, drugged, and humiliated. That was bad enough. But I would make a stand. *I was sodding well not going to go bald! And I was sodding well not going to be called Reggie!* I was going to be me. Thomas the Hirsute. Thomas the Hairy! My future statue would feature a heroic Adonis with a rampant flowing mane, and a faraway look in his eyes. My hands gripped the sides of the basin, as I tried to summon a grim determination from Nobby's soft grey eyes.

I could hear them in the snug. The villagers apparently had teemed through the doorway and crowded round the tiny bar. I opened the door, and the villagers' animated faces froze. They stared. But Thelma Skillet had joined them, and her face was full of love. Her shining eyes melted my heart and my resolve. I ran to her and held her close to me. I even pulled a sniffling Norbert into our huddle. I looked down at them. "Mum and Dad," I whispered. "My *real* Mum and Dad!" And I swayed gently in their arms.

A dozen hankies mopped the eyes and cheeks of a dozen women while their menfolk took refuge at the bar. I wiped away my tears and turned to the little throng.

"I want to thank you all. I never expected this. But–" I took a deep breath. "I'm so happy. Upperthong is my home, and I will love you all as my friends and equals. But Thomas is my name, at least the one on my birth certificate. So, I will be Thomas, ladies and gentlemen. Reverend Thomas!" They all raised their glasses.

"We'll call you Reverend Thomas from now on then, Reggie?" said one old lady.

"Reggie, er Thomas," shouted Gilbert from the bar. "What are you havin'?" I walked to the bar and the huddle of men parted like the Red Sea. I looked at the villagers again.

"Ladies and gentlemen, under the circumstances, there is only one thing I should have. An Upperthong Thunderbolt. And make it a double! Cheers!"

The villagers sprang to their feet, clapping. A gaggle of ladies swarmed about me – hats of straw bedecked with flowers, bobbing butterfly fascinators, grey cloches, exotic jewelled turbans, cheerful beanies and felt fedoras – nudging my cheek as they reached to kiss me. "Reggie! Little Reggie! Lovely boy? Gorgeous chap."

I stood amid the swirl of millinery, dizzy with the scent of Gracie Fields Eau de Toilette and talcum powder. Their gloved hands slipped around my waist, and a camera flashed. A pint glass appeared in my hand.

"Methuselah's Old Wrinkly, Reverend. Finest pint in Thong!" said Gilbert. "Cheers!"

I raised the glass to my lips. The beer smelled hoppy and rich and I drank deeply. I licked my lips. "Cheers, all!" I said.

* * *

Thomas is now my middle name. It's OK.
Like a Labrador, I answer to the call of Reggie.
Now I know who I am.
Nobby has moved in.
Well, there is plenty of room in the vicarage.

Snooker tonight.

JULIAN'S WINGS

Two old friends meet up to see a rock concert

Julian was waiting. He liked to be early. He worried about being late. Then he would be worried because he was early and nobody else had come yet. Then he would think he had got the date wrong. Then he would hunt about for his ticket. This was because he had forgotten I always got the tickets.

As I pushed open the pub door, I saw his ashen face peering over an empty pint glass. Tufts of thinning grey hair shot out from his crown and behind his pink ears. This image was a far cry from Jools, the flame-haired hard-drinking roadie with our school rock band, Dangerous Chihuahuas, who had memorably embarked on a three-day acid and booze binge at his parents' Georgian townhouse in Brighton. A forty-year career, joined umbilically to Apple Macs, had dowsed Julian's fire and drained the fertile swamp of his libido. The Dangerous Chihuahuas had barked their last and long been put down.

"You're late," said Julian.

I looked at my watch. I was two minutes early. "Sorry, Julian."

"You staying in the abyss?" said Julian.

I sighed. "No, the Ibis." Oh no, not *this* joke.

Julian winked. "No. Trust me, John. It's the Abyss."

"It's not that bad," I grinned painfully. Same joke every time. Didn't have the heart to say that I was really staying at the El Paradiso Bed and Breakfast, run by the formidably kaftaned Consuela, in Judas Street. But I had to say the Ibis. Just so Julian could make the same joke. Again. "Fancy a beer?"

"Just had one." He rose from his seat. He was wearing shorts.

"Shorts? It's freezing out there."

"I always wear shorts," he insisted. "I'm going out to do that thing I've given up doing." He winked again. His hand reached into his top pocket and slipped out a packet of cigars. "See. Given up the fags." He smiled, before heading for the door. I watched his chubby, varicose veined legs disappear into the throng. Julian's wife, Fiona, normally joined us on these gigs. She had saved Julian's life when he had a stroke. But she had gone with her friends from the Ladies Aquafit Club to watch *Mamma Mia!* I caught my podgy image in the bar mirror. That was no oil painting, either. Ah well.

Earlier, outside the El Paradiso, I had met Ali, the *Big Issue* seller, standing by a low wall, his pallid face peeping from the hood of his khaki parka. I gave a thumbs-up. "On my way back," I said.

"They always say that!" He stared.

"No, I will. Promise." He shrugged and sat down.

As I had plodded towards The Grumpy Mole to meet Julian, Portsmouth Guildhall came into view. The portentous, neo-classical columns were at odds with the populous and streaming student district of the city, its paved walkways weaving between blocks of grey undergraduate flats and maisonettes. A bearded student was sitting curled in a round window, reading a book. He turned and waved at me as I passed by. I waved back. The city winds shook the alien trees that lined the sidewalks and precincts; Himalayan birches, crimson hawthorns, and bronze Amelanchiers, with leaves like glittering coins, clicking in the autumn breeze.

This gig was another pilgrimage for the grey-pigtailed and corpulent, the fast-aging and anxious sexagenarian masses, huddled in donkey jackets, who had guzzled beer for decades and had now exchanged acid for statins, lustrous manes for ferocious untidy eyebrows and ear hair, Ford Capris for bus passes, roll-ups and reefers for vapers, and Jesus sandals for sensible brogues and walking boots. So why were we coming, converging like a silent army, convening yet again? The reason? Even for someone like me, who couldn't play a note, music had been our constant companion. Our dearest friend. It still was.

And we were coming to hear the rebellious, discordant, psychedelic music of our teens, the music that made our mums and dads shake their heads, slam the door and despair for their post-war dreams. The emergence of Nick Mason's Saucerful of Secrets band was as a reincarnation, the touch of a familiar sun upon our furrowed brow, the kiss of a long-lost lover, the sudden unfolding of leathery and weather-beaten wings. We wanted to fly again.

In the Grumpy Mole, Julian returned with two more pints of Methuselah's Old Wrinkly. "Is there a support act?"

"Emma Tricca. Finger-picker." I took a good draw from my beer. It was hoppy and dry. I wiped my lips. "She's playing her new album. *St. Peter.*"

"Oh," said Julian. He sipped his beer. There was a burst of horsey laughter from the next table. Julian raised one eyebrow. "Listen to those buggers!"

A man wearing a steampunk top hat embellished with a feather, goggles, and an array of Pink Floyd badges was holding court. As if addressing the Bloomsbury Set over canapés and Chablis rather than Nobby's Nuts and Best Bitter, he relentlessly name-dropped rock stars whom he seemed to know as personal friends. Two other companions were sitting with their backs to us: two bald pates, with pigtails beneath that shook and trembled as they chortled.

A slender woman sitting at the end of the table, in a long Afghan coat, rocked back in her chair, planting her Doc Martin boots on the table. Her hair flowed in timeless rivulets of platinum, granite, and silver, streaming across her shoulders. Seemingly detached from Top Hat's peroration, she beamed as someone who had seen it all and yet judged no one. The retroussé nose, laughing eyes, and elegant mouth seemed to evoke the period of the music we had come to applaud and venerate. But Top Hat had embarked on another yarn, and the pigtails swung once more.

"Gawd sake!" said Julian, shaking his head. "What a row! Let's go."

* * *

Julian and I huddled in the queue along the wall of the Guildhall.

"Have you got the tickets?" Julian gave me an anxious stare.

"I just gave you yours."

"Oh, shit!" Julian rummaged in his black donkey jacket. He grasped the crumpled ticket triumphantly and grinned. "See. I'm not losing it."

I smiled and averted my head from yet another cloud of vapour from the man in front. The pungent scent of weed drifted among the shuffling column of conker-shoed and booted musical followers. Some had mined the depths of their wardrobes and attics to dress for the occasion. The woman in front of me and her partner sported psychedelic catsuits, which they amply filled, beneath their Afghan waistcoats, purple hippy wigs and NHS spectacles. Two more were alarmingly dressed in black military tunics with red crossed-hammer armbands and police caps. One tall, thin man peered out from a Kusary black hoodie. The slogan across his chest read I HATE PINK FLOYD but the band name had been crossed out and THE SEX PISTOLS stitched just above. For the rest, it was a varied uniform of fleeces, Padders shoes, stretch-fit comfort jeans, denim waistcoats and faded Floyd T-shirts.

We trudged up the marble staircase and emerged into the auditorium; we claimed our seats in the circle. I had dragged a reluctant Julian from the bar – "Warm-up acts are always crap, anyway" he protested. But I insisted on getting our money's worth and, clutching our beers, we gazed down on an array of percussion and guitars as if abandoned by their players.

The auditorium lights went down, and I experienced that sense of transformation one feels when a show is about to begin. As in a drama, the players know the script. The audience doesn't. It is like placing your hand on the classroom door handle. You know what you are going to say. The children don't. I used to get excited at school, sitting in a lesson, waiting for the teacher to arrive and the door to open. To walk through that door is to be changed by the eyes of those watching. I had that same feeling of excitement now. And a man with a guitar and a woman with black boots and a storm of black hair had walked on to the stage.

"This is Jason. I love writing songs with him." I will not attempt a narration of the concert. Watching a performance is to walk into a stranger's dream, their inner space, willingly and submissively as the musicians search your mind for the touchstones of connection and empathy. I cannot report truthfully and accurately on all of that. Time needs to pass. But around me, the babble had ceased, phones were put away and Julian was sitting on the edge of his seat, his elbows on his knees and fingers tapping thoughtfully on his lips. As was I.

Each song was as a fresh wave breaking and I slipped and swirled within its silver layers. Lyrics matter to me, and I strained to listen; my head went for a walk around the city walls, the West End stores and south suburbs, and paced behind the Sunday walkers, tracing their steps of doubt as another day turned its back. I 'came here to feel', and the pristine and shimmering guitar-playing glittered as light on an unravelling breaker. *Fireghost* brought unease and fear of the watching lighthouse keeper and the deep worry we share that no one is watching the watchers. And it was over. And, as ever, I felt altered. And could not explain how.

Watching *A Saucerful of Secrets*, superlatively played, was to revisit the irreverent ripping up of the fabric of my gawky, insecure fifteen-year-old landscape, where everything was held together by flimsy safety pins, and the foundations of life constantly echoed to the sounds of thunder. As a pallid, wide-eyed schoolboy, I had felt like a sapling in a howling gale, and the sheer punk audacity of the music snatched me, like a poltergeist, back to the shaking and ground-shift of those days. But the closing bars of A Saucerful of Secrets led us to a graceful Dartmoor upland, with the sun rising over Westcombe beach.

Julian and I did not speak as we walked down the stairs and out into the bracing sea air of the port city. We shook hands under the statue of Queen Victoria. "That Emma Whatsit was blooming good."

I nodded. "She certainly was."

"Gotta go, mate," said Julian, his face pale in the lamplight.

"Alright, Julian." His eyes looked small and blank, and I wondered if he was in pain. "Go carefully. Give my love to Fiona." He stumped away into the darkness. I feared for Julian and wondered if I would see him again.

I turned up my coat collar. Another beer in The Grumpy Mole? The place was rammed with concert goers, some standing outside vaping. But that sense of having been transformed in some nameless way made me want to be alone. I pulled out my phone and ordered the Emma Tricca album, St Peter. I wanted to see the lyrics.

I ascended the steps by the Central Library and gazed down the length of The Mary Rose Way. The neon sign of the El Paradiso flickered at the corner of Judas Street. Some stragglers remained in the pavement-side eateries and bars; students on bicycles criss-crossed the square, weaving a matrix between solitary souls and pedestrian clusters. They seemed to be connecting everything. I lifted my eyes to the night sky's roof of stars that had bloomed into shimmering symmetry, and a wind gust shifted the trees, gathering bundles of the Amelanchiers' bronze leaves and hurling them upward, like the wings of a million insects, taking random flight and swirling in the lamplight and the white gaze of the rising moon. As the leaves settled and the wind quietened, I could see Ali sitting at the far end of the boulevard under the Victorian streetlamp. Still on the low wall.

I passed the round window in the student house. The young man now had a girl with him. They raised their beer cans by way of a toast. I liked that. I did not know them and would probably never speak to them, but our life journeys had passed close and touched, like a feather, like the wings of a moth touching down randomly, the world interconnecting through unrelated parallel events. Wings, touching down.

"You came back," said Ali.

"Of course." I sat down next to him on the wall.

"So many don't."

"But I did. And you were here. So, you kept your promise too. Thanks." I smiled and reached into my jacket pocket. "Anyway. I need to chat. Here's my £2.50."

Ali looked at me. His face was younger than I thought. He had a fine face with dark eyebrows. There was a scar on his cheek. We had chatted a few times before. I had seen him at the Folk Club.

He took the coins, dug into his bag, and pulled out a copy of *The Big Issue*. There was a picture of the actor Jodie Whittaker, who was taking over the role of Doctor Who. "Heroes keep coming in new forms," shouted the red strapline, with an image of the Tardis whirling off into deep space. "That's very appropriate," I said. Ali nodded approvingly. I sighed and stared back down the street. The cyclists had disappeared, and the groups of people were thinning, drifting into the ghostly lanes and shadowy doorways. But the stars seemed to be moving, rising, and enlarging, their hues and tints changing.

"El Paradiso!" exclaimed Ali.

"Right now, Ali, it is. Believe me, it is." Often, I need someone else to perceive truths, to light the lamps along the pathway. Like the students in the round window. But Ali was looking at Consuela; she was standing smoking a cigarette outside the El Paradiso, in her orange kaftan with her hand on her hip, staring in a pose that reminded me of a sangria jug.

"You're wanted, John," said Ali, smiling. There was a ping on my phone. I touched the screen. The lyrics of *Julian's Wings* had appeared. I murmured them slowly.

Across the borderline of a painted smile,
Blue eyes are filtering stories in Kodak Chrome
Glimpses of glasses—reflections from another time
Colours a-flashing when Julian's wings are touching down

Ali was smiling at me, as if at a child. "You OK, John?"

"I'm fine Ali." I breathed deeply. I was thinking of Julian. "Had my tree shaken a bit, that's all."

"Mine shakes all the time," Ali said. "It's better that way. You need some wings."

I nodded. "Yes, Ali. I do."

Julian's Wings is from the album *St. Peter* by Emma Tricca (Dell'Orso Records).

OM

A schoolboy is befriended by Om - his smartphone - and Monty, the village cat

Picture an English garden. Level lawn freshly cut. A shiver of autumn shaking the fronds of oaks and elms, their emerald leaves tinged with russet. The dead heads of roses and chrysanthemums uncut, awaiting execution. The first gatherings of dry leaves scuttling like rodents across the grey terrace and clustering in dead bundles beneath the grey stone steps or floating on the ornamental pond like abandoned ships and castaways.

Come with me now. Stand with me beneath the branch of the oak tree. Turn your head. See the glittering ocean at Wyscombe, its waves unravelling in curling and curving sea surges. Catch the sound of its shingle clatter and the sucking, shrinking, shifting of grinding gravel, sea stones and debris of splintered wood. On that beach at Wyscombe is a block of oak, bigger than your bed; its sea-scoured surface bears the cuts of axe head and sword. Its voice is ancient. Listen.

See the ruined Dream Factory, its seaward wall bearing the shattered fireplace, the hearth where children sat and dreamt and felt safe and held each other in a crucible of hope. The stones that composed its wall are scattered, like the heads of martyrs, on the tussocky bank of Wyscombe brook, or lay blankly staring upward from the bounding stream's rushing bed.

Turn now. The wind shudders the patient woodland and dry leaves swirl, their desiccated slivers spinning to the forest floor. Look back to the house of granite and stout medieval timbers. There is Peter Young, sitting on a thin wooden chair; his elbows on the table, a chessboard between him and the battle-scarred village cat.

* * *

Monty stared back across the table. For Peter, to look at Monty was to feel a bond of faith and knowledge that he could not explain. There still, the yellow eyes, probing stare, and tiger stripes. What wordless message was this creature imparting to Peter on the eve of his journey to find his parents? Peter concentrated hard. Was he imbibing through mere eye-contact some wisdom, some feline intuition, a set of truths defining his course of action? He did not know, but the longer he looked, the deeper his well of certainty.

Peter had found a dog-eared essay written by his father; he had read *Annica: a Study* slowly, negotiating his way through scrawled handwriting, coffee rings, smudges of cigarette ash and, he suspected, beer stains. He had finished reading and had arrived at the shores of reason. He sat back, watching a hawk carving brilliant lines and arcs in the bright sky.

"Everything is in a constant state of change, nothing is permanent," he murmured to the autumn air. This made sense. He stared at Monty again, the yellow eyes and peculiar peppered nose.

"We do not matter, Monty," he said. Monty blinked. "The chessboard is order. To move the pieces is to create suffering." *I could stay here*, he thought. He felt the train ticket in his pocket. *But I have to go.* A vision of playing chess with his father rose before his eyes.

"You can't take the king, Peter. You must not kill the king." His father had smiled.

"But I have won." Peter had said.

His father tipped the black king on its side. "I am leaving the field, Peter. You have won. Don't kill the king. There is no need to." Peter saw the gentle enquiring eyes of his father; he had placed his spectacles on the table and smiled.

"No need to kill the idea." The vision shivered and departed. Peter shivered too, a stab of pain at the memory of his lost parents; he could feel a smouldering intent and anger at war with his suffering.

"Monty. I have to put the king and queen back on their spaces." Monty gazed. "I have to."

Peter had found other treasures of student life in John and Esther's study. Love letters from 'Victoria', a crude birthday card from 'Roger' showing a sketch of male genitalia sporting a pair of purple sunglasses, a photo of John and Esther at a student party, dressed as Jarvis Cocker and Ginger Spice. John sported oversize, chunky plastic glasses, a Cool Britannia T-shirt and the green Goth jacket that he had given to Peter. Esther's red wig flared and sprang, startled, her Union Jack dress not quite concealing her equally patriotic knickers.

There were other discoveries: a ticket for a Parrotheads gig, a purple wallet of battered CDs (Automatic for The People, Different Class), a newspaper cutting about Esther winning a prize for physics (on the back, something about a dead princess), crumbling marijuana in a round Ogden's tin, an Einstein doll with wild hair and staring eyes.

Peter had carefully arranged these curiosities – the chess pieces of his parents' life – on his father's desk. Jarvis Cocker and Ginger Spice had pride of place, colourfully occupying the thrones of power. Peter smiled down at these eclectic memorabilia. Was this what being at university was like? Buddhism and Cool Britannia, the Astra Prize for Physics and Union Jack pants. Now in his garden, the early evening sun descending – a blinding red orb above Wyscombe, a symphony of blood-crimson, peach and burnt umber – Peter mused. *How little he had known.* Strange. Peter's eyes turned to Om, the intel-unit Esther had designed. A shimmer of purple light flowed over Om's elliptical surface.

"Om, I want you to take a really good picture of Monty."

"What do you mean *really* good? Of Monty? That's not possible."

"No. A picture of *him*. See what I see."

"Well, if the Master of All He Surveys will deign to

keep still." Om projected a vertical point of light. It was the length of your forearm. At its tip, a concentrated beam rotated ninety degrees and faced Monty. In a blink it was done, and Monty's image – not entirely free of vanity – flooded Om's surface.

"Any good?" said Om.

"Got it," said Peter. "That is him. That is who he is."

"*What* he is."

"No, *who* he is. *Who*, Om. Remember that. I might need him."

"On your journey? You might," agreed Om. "You are meeting Navinda at midday. Don't forget."

"Ben Crouch's Café. How could I?"

Peter placed Om in his pocket and walked through the silent dusk into his home. He stood in the hall. He smiled at the old cardboard suit of armour guarding the stairs; he and Dad had made it for the village pantomime. The soft contours of the house, its oak bookshelves lined with volumes – jackets of old leather and gaudy paperbacks, and big picture-books; Peter's school exercise books and those of his parents jostled for space in a creaking mahogany bookcase by the stairs.

As he ascended, he gazed at the vivid photographs John and Esther had accumulated on their travels, framed romantically with knotty driftwood studded with coloured glass and seashells. The supernatural steaming chasms of Rotorua and sacred waters of the lake; at Cape Farewell, Mum and Dad had said, you could feel a sense of departure from this planet just by sitting on the strange, vast seashell spit, curving like a divine arc of light to enclose the ethereal calm of Golden Bay.

Peter pictured himself swimming with Navinda, with the seals and dolphins in the warm waters, the burning sun hung in a cobalt sky. They would then sit on the beach of shells and talk, the light glancing off her storm of black hair. He closed his eyes to hold on to the dream a moment longer. One day. "One day," he murmured.

Peter studied his image in the bathroom mirror, the tousled hair, ragged green jacket and restless eyes. Peter cleaned his teeth and washed his face, all the while pondering his appearance and who he was. He could hear the steady tick of the Victorian longcase clock in the hall. It felt like the beating of his pulse. Steady, regular, patient, eternal and oddly timeless. Without his parents, there seemed to be no time. There was no one to tell him to get up, tidy his room, fetch the logs, run the dogs; no one to raise a critical eyebrow if he used a bad word, or complain about the length of his fingernails, his untidy mop of fair hair, wearing odd socks, or had he done his homework? His life was suddenly unregulated and robbed of its rhythm and beating heart.

He walked across to his bed and placed Om on the bedside table. So, what should he do? What was right? He sat up in bed with a glass of milk, flicking through the pages of Dad's essay while Om glowed. Monty had slipped into the bedroom and settled comfortably on Peter's jacket which he had hurled onto a chair. Once again, he recalled his parents' violent abduction with a shudder. Monty and Om were Peter's only companions since the police left.

"Have I shown you my latest trick?" Om glowed a soft purple.

"Go on. Impress me." Peter eased himself upright in his bed.

Om projected the beam of light once more. At its peak it fanned out and pointed towards the silent bedroom door. A shifting spectral image formed slowly in the soft light. Peter concentrated hard. Magically, he was looking at Navinda. The black jacket. The blue jeans. Her dark hair. He had met her on a school trip. Navinda had smiled shyly, melting Peter's heart, when he took her photograph. Om was using the picture.

Peter gasped. "I love Navinda," he blurted.

"Love?" said Om.

The word had flown from his lips and seemed to hover in the air. "Yes," he said softly. Om glowed. Peter breathed.

Stillness returned. "Om, can you make her speak?" He glanced at the elliptical disk on his bedside table. The alarm clock ticked. It was late.

"No, not yet. But meet Navinda's friend." Om shimmered, and a myriad of colours projected into the dark space. Peter saw himself emerge from his bedroom door and stand, the green Goth jacket, bird's nest of hair, black scruffy jeans and carelessly laced boots. The image turned to Navinda and smiled.

"Perfect. Amazing, Om."

"I like to please," said Om.

"Except ..."

"Ah, 'except'! Now for the criticism."

"No, Om, it's brilliant." Peter gazed at the images, marvellously detailed, firm, strong – not shifting or floating. "Incredible."

"But?" said Om.

"The scar on my forehead. My bike accident." He stifled a yawn.

He placed Om back on the table and gasped as the holograms dissipated into the darkness. He shivered and looked pleadingly at Om.

"Get some sleep," said Om. "You have a long journey tomorrow. If that dim-witted alarm clock doesn't wake you up, I will."

Peter lay his head on the pillow. "It's just that ..."

"I know," said Om. "Remember. I am here to look after you. Don't forget that."

Peter thought of the shattered Dream Factory, the family's stone cottage on Wystcombe Beach, where, until now, he had spent every day. And when he was not there, he had dreamt of being there. He sighed.

"It's not so bad without Mum and Dad."

Om glowed blue. A single beam of light travelled across the walls and illuminated some of Peter's hastily dabbed landscapes.

"I like that one," said Om.

"Wyscombe. From the sea. I used one of Dad's photographs." The light drifted on and came to rest, a gentle pool enveloping Peter's face.

"Why is it not so bad?" said Om.

Peter considered the matter, staring into the gentle centre of the light. "I know them so much better now."

REPTILES

A writer takes the train to London

August had burnished the green meadows into dazzling gold; fields of maize and wheat furrowed and furled as the winds played among the shifting ranks of cornstalks. Peter Young will take this same train journey, I mused, and scribbled some notes on my tablet. I recall now the secret smile that must have played across my lips in that moment. Peter Young will take this same journey to find himself – as I was.

Skuas and sandpipers darted like jets above silent inland ponds and grassy dunes, resplendent with juniper and shimmering mosses of maidenhair and pointed spear. The roly-poly golfers, colourfully attired, waddling across Dawlish Warren, were of passing comic fascination – *dinosaurs on vacation*, I noted. As the train trembled and swayed along the estuary rim, I pondered the message on my phone: "Sorry I can't make it, old boy. Prime minister in a tizzy. Gave my ticket to an old friend. He wants to meet you. Enjoy the match."

I always liked to travel on my own – preferring the company of strangers on a journey. Peter and his girlfriend, Navinda Eman, are the characters from The Dream Factory. Both aged seventeen; you could call it a coming-of-age love story. Peter is like me: idle, only switches on when it suits him. Navinda, from a Palestinian family, determined, focused, formidably intelligent. But I had to put Navinda together as a character – I had never met anyone quite like her. So far. And I was struggling for a theme. For all the unrolling of chapters, and unfurling of landscape and words, it had to be about … well … *something*.

The train slow-turned and accelerated. I felt the excitement, the momentum of change.

The waves rolled up the estuary; the train surged beyond them and struck across country, the arteries of rivers and motorways sliding beneath as we traversed bridges and swept along embankments. I shook out my newspaper. The pope's visit to London was coming. I snorted. I had no time for movements, clubs, sects, organised religions, and yet, I had to admit, the idea of faith preoccupied me. *My* journey, I knew, was one of faith but where would it take me? Did it matter? But religious leaders? No way. Count me out.

A student looked up from the essay she'd been writing on the table opposite me. Her cocoa-brown eyes stared at me through round glasses; a stud shone from her nose, and a tattoo appeared to be sliding its fiery fingers across her shoulder. "Can I look?" she enquired.

"Of course." I slid the newspaper across. She refolded it to display the whole article. Her fingers followed the text and she grunted.

"Stupid old bastard!" she exclaimed. A woman looked up from her novel, and a smart-suited young man next to me lowered his phone. She read more. "Yeah, right on." She stood up. "Listen to this, folks." All heads turned to look as the colour drained from my face. "Listen to this! It's cool! 'The pope's opposition to condoms kills people. It is all very well – his lecturing us on morals – but he should look at his own organisation. He will be met with the most utter, exquisite, grovelling politeness, and with that, somehow we're in an uncivilised third world country.' Ain't that the truth!"

As the young woman's tirade continued, my body shrunk and shrivelled like a leaf in the fire.

She waved a bangled arm in the air. "Oh, there's more. 'What is civilised about demeaning women, demonising homosexuals, wishing that IVF children had never been born? Our only crime has been silence.'" By this time my toes were curling up inside my shoes; a bead of sweat rolled down my brow. This girl stood there, bold and defiant, daring fellow passengers to disagree. A burst of applause came from the seat behind me and was picked up by others farther down the coach. The older woman had shrunk back to her novel. I closed my eyes. *This will be over soon*, I thought.

"But we must have leaders," the man next to me piped up, prolonging my agony.

The student fixed him in his seat, her hands on her hips in a gesture that reminded me of a Victorian teapot. "Yes, but wouldn't it be nice to have a pope – if we must have one – who isn't totally bloody embarrassing?" He visibly withered under her stare.

She sat down slowly, absorbing the trembling silence that had descended on the passengers. Her eyes found me again. "Do you agree with that?" Her finger jabbed the newspaper once again, before she slid it back across the table. *Oh, lord, she's still going*, I thought. "Do you?"

Inside me something turned over; I felt naked. "Until just now, I didn't know." I breathed deeply. Best to be honest, but what did I really believe? She continued to stare at me. "I also think we must have leaders ..." Her eyes flickered, and her lips began to form a response. "We must have leaders." She raised an eyebrow. "And ... I think I've just met one. I'm glad you said what you did."

My hesitancy wasn't because I didn't trust any political group or faith; it was because I didn't have the courage to be wrong. It was fear. I admired this student because she wasn't afraid; she would stare threats in the face. Like Peter. Like Navinda. I felt humbled. "You remind me of two young people I know ..." I trailed off, averting my eyes. "Two young friends of mine."

"I would like to meet them," she said.

"Not possible."

"Not possible?"

"No."

"Why?"

I shook my head. "Hard to explain." I looked away.

The student resumed her essay, scribbling rapidly and periodically flipping the pages of her notepad. She seized her phone and scrolled through her messages. "You realise we won't meet again." She looked at me quizzically. "What are the odds of that happening?"

I pondered briefly. "Seven million to one?"

She smiled. "More than that. More than when we got on this train."

"I'll let you do the maths."

"The thing is," she continued, fixing me once again with her eyes, "I believe you have to seize the moment. You must speak up. Not to say anything is a crime. Don't you agree?" She placed her eyeglasses on the table and removed a clasp from the back of her head; her dark hair tumbled about her shoulders. Who is this girl? Do I know her? I knew I did, but I couldn't explain how. "I'm sorry if I embarrassed you."

I shook my head. "I wasn't embarrassed."

"You were." She chuckled. "I could tell."

"No." But I was feeling embarrassed now.

"You went red. Then you looked out the window."

I smiled. "You found me out." I was praying I would not blush again.

The train slid into London's Paddington station, the curved platforms slipping like fingers on either side of the train. The student stood up and pulled down her rucksack, shoving her notepad and book into the pack. Then she unzipped a side pocket for her phone.

The train came to a stop. I stood up and retrieved my newspaper and bag. I extended my hand. "Goodbye." The girl smiled and shook my hand. I felt her cool, slender fingers in my palm and shivered.

"Goodbye," she said. "Talking is good. Without it, there is no truth. Nothing changes." Was this happening to me? The hairs on the back of my neck rose. "Don't you agree?" She drew the straps of her pack across her shoulders and joined the passenger queue shuffling down the train. I stood there, gaping and foolish. The queue shuffled forward; she looked back fleetingly and smiled. I glanced down at the table. There was scrap of paper. She had written, "The man who never alters his opinions is like standing water, and breeds reptiles of the mind."

"You all right, chief?"

I turned. The carriage was empty. The student had gone. I had met Navinda, and she had left me with the precious gift of a theme.

The ticket collector stood in his grey uniform, his glasses glinting above a broad smile. "The train terminates 'ere, Guv."

BANQUO'S GHOST

A teacher is haunted by a mysterious classroom incident

It is strange when a book becomes a living thing, lifts off the page, and you have to write about the characters, or you feel they might become neglected or fade or decay or lose limbs or potency. I feel sorry for having reached this point and tried stupidly to be inscrutable, pretend not to be there, as if I cannot endure the thought of you knowing who I am – offering only a modicum of duty to you by just including short glimpses into the light and shadows of my life.

There is no mystery to who I am in your world, but in mine … well, that is why I am writing this, to make sense of it all. I want to wake up one day and know. I want to know there is another, better truth. The only way to do that is to push open the doorway into the dark.

The more I write, the more the characters begin to live, become people I admire and have affection for. Love. What has happened to make that happen, to be unable to live without them? I can't go on a train or bus or walk through the school playground without seeing them; I have long conversations, and they strip layers from my artifice and leave me with nothing. They demand honesty. They can be brutal. Fear stalks me, and they know it and use it. They can hurt me deeply, as only those closest to you can.

Sometimes I panic about neglecting characters or feel they may be hurt, or they want to be done with things and abandon me. I feel guilty while taking assembly, holding a meeting, or having lunch, or striding through the corridors, or speaking to children, meeting worried parents, taking money out of the bank, cleaning my teeth, or tending my greenhouse. The guilt is always waiting, tapping on my brain, catching my eye in a mirror, or moving past the surgery window as the doctor checks my pulse. Or Savaric – my ghost-friend –

appears to remind me with a knowing smile. One day, their honesty might kill me.

A scene or a place leaps out of my past. I panic, have to write it, visit the place, embrace and wrestle with the ghosts that populate its shadowy streets and alleys and strange land of skeletal trees and misty fields.

The Old School has arisen: a mirage of dull square buildings and rickety teaching huts. Let's drive there! My memory is charged with shifting images and pictures of the rooms and spaces, the children I taught – a cast of characters, now departed.

I really need you now. So, keep close. This will not be easy.

I had expected to see its buildings whole and strong. I knew it had closed. Something terrible had happened. Parents had taken their children away.

I expected to see deserted classrooms, the old assembly hall with its gleaming floor, lines of coat hooks, wire trays, and book heaps stacked high, some toppled. Old RMs and BBC Masters blank and broken, innards yanked out and smashed; the giant roller chalkboards bearing only graffiti and crude scrawlings of genitalia. The noisy Octagon, team lists pinned to corkboards, rolls of honour, and toilets pungent with fag smoke and urine. Outside the silent staff room, the memorial garden gently tended. I even checked on Google Earth to see if it was all still there. I had expected to see these things.

Our car passes along the concrete avenues of avuncular semis and gaunt maisonettes. Dreary Victory Flats, an ashen cold-war relic, drifts by, its stark square silhouette dimming the weak sunlight. But now we walk towards the chain-link fence. A red sign: *site closed, no access.*

There is a dog hole in the wire. Come with me. Let us see.

There, an old concrete streetlamp, light smashed, a pointless relic amid the desolation. Desultory boys used to congregate beneath it and smoke. Everything has gone, each stone ground down to a sterile shingle of concrete and brick. See the dead bonfires of charred drawings and exercise books; chair legs, like hacked-off limbs, protrude from skips. The memorial garden has been bulldozed, its bonsais and saplings snapped, and vehicle tracks snakeskin across its floral beds and sculpted lawns. The little plaques of commemoration are crushed and twisted, flower garlands and wreaths snatched up by reptilian JCBs to be scrunched and minced. Lines of skips, like tanks, await evacuation beneath circles of wheeling gulls and crows.

One low brick wall survives. I used to drink my coffee here, and kids would gather with their crisps to chat while footballs thudded against the tennis-court fence. Follow the footpath to the end and look! Class 3W gathers around and sweeps as a wave into room seventeen, as the sea floods the rock fissures in Fairyland. The room always bore the stench of wax and disinfectant; there was a baited rattrap by the door.

Place your hand on the classroom door handle. When you do, everything you planned to do morphs. The lesson you had schemed is snatched from your pocket by a piskie. I've always known that from the very first time. I used to get excited at school, sitting in a lesson, waiting for the teacher to arrive and the door to open. To walk through that door is to transform who you are, to walk through the wardrobe, to cross the river, to open the trapdoor. Try it.

I remember. Class 3W flowed into the room: twenty-nine heads facing front, senses switched on, minds alight. I handed out twenty-nine copies of Macbeth. "Not enough, sir. One more needed."

Baffled, I rooted out a spare. "OK, act three, scene four, the banquet scene." I looked around the room. Fifteen pairs of seats; there should be one spare.

I took a paper register. Twenty-nine "Here, sir." No "She's away. She's miching." Unusual. There should be one spare seat. I looked up. There were none.

"Is anyone here who shouldn't be? Has anyone come to the wrong room?"

"None of us wants to be here, sir." Laughter.

"No one wants you here, Elvis; you stink." Laughter.

"OK, OK. Let's get on." I paced the room as we read the text. This was getting to me. I stared at each child then looked across the room, expecting to see their double. They all had exercise books. There should have been one without.

When we did the part where Macbeth goes mad, I was reading the lines aloud. My voice didn't sound like my voice.

"Bit loud, sir!"

"Sssh! Sir's acting!"

I ended the lesson early. "Cor, cheers, sir!"

"Leave your books by the door."

I won't tell you how many books were in the pile. You know, don't you?

The senior mistress told me off for letting the class out early. "You'll never make a teacher." She shook her head.

At the end of the afternoon, I sat in the staff room, staring across the fields to Victory Flats. I couldn't talk to anyone about what I'd seen. I would have to live with it.

I refused to teach in that room again. I said I was allergic to polish.

Savaric, the ghost, said I shouldn't have been afraid. It had happened before. I just hadn't noticed.

51

FUNNY OLDE ENGLISHE

A schoolboy discovers a new word....

Perhaps even at the age of seven, I began to think my life was unreal. Not like others. Swallows and Amazons and The Adventures of Mr. Toad and My First Book of Poetry – even the bewildering visits to the church – all spoke of the lives of happy families enjoying picnics in the sun.

My mother and sister were shouting. I remember a full mug of hot tea flying across the kitchen, almost in slow motion, before it struck the wall above my mother and its scalding contents rained upon her new perm.

Later, I was lying in bed, and mum stood woozily at my door, holding a wineglass.

"Do you know what your sister called me?"

I feigned sleep.

"She called me a bawd." Mother wobbled slightly as I half opened my eyes. "Do you know what a bawd is?"

Of course, I knew what a board was. But why on earth call her that? Oh, well, a board is made of wood, like a plank; that sounded more promising. But Mother was not giving me any more time to pursue this fascinating theory.

"A bawd is a woman of the streets."

My image of a plank was replaced by a strange scene of a street occupied by grey women dressed like my grandmother.

"A prostitute! She called me a prostitute!"

Now I really was confused. I knew what a substitute was. I was twelfth man for the school's cricket team and occasionally went on the field as a substitute. Perhaps a prostitute was a superior form of substitute. If I practised my batting and bowling really hard, I might be promoted to be a prostitute. "Prostitute." I murmured the word so as to remember it.

The next day I went to school and looked up the word in my First English Dictionary. But it wasn't there. Perhaps I'd got the spelling wrong. "Sir," I said brightly to Mr. Moore, my English teacher, "How do you spell 'prostitute'?"

Mr. Moore's eyebrows levitated above the rim of his spectacles. He gave me a long stare. "It's just that my mother …" My words petered out.

Mr. Moore was chewing his lower lip thoughtfully, and then he spluttered, "Excuse me, class." He raced for the classroom door. A boy said he had heard someone laughing in the staff gents.

I found out what it meant. In the playground. And several other words. From now on a tart wasn't merely something made of pastry.

WILMOTT

A memory from school days...

Wilmott was a bully. He had a shock of dark hair, and dark brown eyes. He was suntanned and wore polished football boots. He was fine-boned and agile. He had a smart leather wallet. There was a photo of a girl in it. He stood upright and confident. He would speak to the masters ingratiatingly and mock them behind their backs. He gathered power without breaking sweat. He knew what to say. A handsome raven with crows as sidekicks. Others would do his dirty work.

"You, Simes. See that boy's school cap stuck in his bag. Steal it, boy!"

The boy was sitting on a brick wall with his friends, eating sandwiches. Trembling inside, I strolled past the little group of first years, snatched the cap and ran back to Wilmott, who was grinning.

"I say, boys. Did you see what that rascal Simes did?" he shouted. The first years all looked up. "He stole your cap! What a little thief, a sneaky little magpie he is! He was going to hide it in the bogs!" I dropped the cap and ran. I hid in the library.

Willmott was a prefect. He was a dinner monitor. He was in charge when the plump dinner lady put the food on the trestle table. He and his friends would take most of the pie, the best meat and mash, and all the gravy. Then it would be pudding.

"Tapioca, boys! What a treat!" He grinned and started scooping the slop into the plastic bowls. "But wait a moment, boys. There is something to add. Plum jam!" he oozed. "Delicious!" he said, smacking his lips. "A nice big blob for everyone! There!" He dolloped the red jam into each bowl, making a crimson spot in the centre. "Some for everyone, except ..." He looked at me, grinning. "Except for Simes. Look at how pathetic he is, wearing his uniform like a sack, looking like the *thief* he is!"

He stood grinning as my blood ran cold and the boys' faces turned to look at me. Some were smiling. Some just looked afraid. In that moment, I knew that one day I would be avenged. I would have my moment.

I stood up and walked to the end of the table. I looked down at the smirking Wilmott. The dining hall went silent. The headmaster – Mr Gooley – in his long-sleeved robe, stood on the dais like a hapless woodcock, watching. I wanted to punch Wilmott but dared not.

Four years later. Special assembly. Wilmott had been heroic. A fine example. A House Captain. A leader among men. But he had died in a car crash. His mother, tearful, shook hands with Mr Gooley, accepting the gift of a carriage clock. The masters stood sombrely in their black gowns. A wake of vultures.

"You remember what a bully he was?" a boy whispered. "Took his dad's flash car. Always drove too fast."

It shocked me.

How little we pitied him.

I WALKED THE BEACH WITH YOU LAST NIGHT

Peter and Navinda hide in the cellar

P eter hurled his green jacket onto the carved oak chair at the foot of the stairs. "Yvonne wants us to hide. The only place I can think of is the cellar. At least we can lock ourselves in."

Navinda was looking at the bookshelves in the hall. She immediately loved the wood-panelled walls and photographs of Venice Beach and Golden Bay that ascended the staircase. "Are these your schoolbooks?" She pulled three exercise books from the shelf and read the covers. "Peter Young, Essays," she announced. "And what have we here? Peter Young. Poetry! These are books I must read if I am to know who you really are." She beamed at Peter. He took her hand.

"This way." They walked to the end of the hall, where Peter unlocked a door. It swung inwards, and Navinda saw wooden steps leading into the cellar. Peter turned off the hall light and closed the door. He then reached for a long cord and tugged it. A soft light gently illuminated the cellar.

"It's warm down here," said Navinda. She flung her leather jacket on to a wooden chair.

"That's because of the heating boiler."

Navinda surveyed the wooden beams, and the plastered walls, the wine rack beneath the steps, a stack of suitcases, oak shelves laden with box files and documents bundled together with red string. There were other treasures: a rack of old cricket bats, their blades oiled to the colour of aged leather, pairs of football boots strung on hooks, gleaming petanque sets, and a timber box of odd gardening gloves, sunhats and boots. A wooden rocking horse, its once proud mane now reduced to ragged tufts of wool, sat motionless; the boxed train set, a battered dolls' house, and bikes chained together against the wall. She stopped by the bed. "All your life is in this room, Peter."

"Yes. I used to play here with my friends when I was young. I was down here when Mum and Dad were taken."

"Why?"

"My room was being decorated. All finished now."

"A very romantic place to bring a girl, Peter Young. I hope you have brought no others down here. I would be very upset to know that!"

"No, no, I have n-never ..." Peter stammered. "No one else. I promise." He gazed at Navinda – her eyes were full of light. "Sorry. Erm ... I don't know what to say. Oh, I need to lock the door."

"I'll do it!" Navinda turned and walked across the cellar. Peter loved to see the rhythmic elegance of her movement. She turned the key in the lock and slid the bolts across. "There. Are we safe now?"

Peter nodded. "We should be."

"You know what to say now."

Peter looked perplexed. "Sorry?"

"A moment ago, you said you didn't know what to say."

"I still don't, really... I'm trembling."

"But you know what to say when you're writing in these books." She held up his book of poetry.

"Sometimes I write down here. It feels good in this room."

Navinda looked across to a small wooden desk by the door. An anglepoise lamp was clamped to the edge. A piece of paper lay on the blotter pad, and an italic pen protruded from a glass inkwell. She walked across. "May I?"

Peter winced. "Oh, crikey!"

"Your writing is beautiful." Navinda slid off her black boots and socks. The wooden floorboards were smooth and cool to her bare feet. She smiled. "I want this room to touch my skin. I want to be a part of this room." She walked slowly, softly reading the poem aloud.

I walked the beach with you last night,
heard the kiss and sigh of the waves far out,
watched the sea unfurl in layers of glass across the
sand,
saw the stars reflect like pearls,
while our moon held court. Sometimes
I want to walk blindly out into the dark,
keep walking on and on under the splendour of the
stars.
I stare up at them like a child.

The beast has retreated to the silent trees,
crucifixes on the skyline.
Shadows depart from behind these rocks;
winter relents its grip before the dance of spring.

I walked on the beach with you last night,
watched the waters slip, slide like silken sheets.
Under this cathedral roof of stars
I make a promise never to lie,
never to dim the brightness of your eyes.
I will make a pillow of these starlit sands,
my heart, a pearl, in your loving hands.

Navinda paused and breathed deeply. She placed the poem back on the desk and turned to face Peter.

"It's not very good. I'm still working on it," he said. Peter cringed whenever his teachers read his work aloud. He felt emotionally naked.

"Do you always handwrite your work?"

"Mum gave me an italic pen when I started school. She said the pen is the most powerful weapon in the world. Something like that."

"The poem's quite good," said Navinda, her eyes shining. "What is this beast you mentioned?"

"It's … it's … fear."

"You are afraid? After all we have been through?"

"Yes." Peter shook. "I'm afraid of not fitting in. Of not knowing what to do. I feel like a fool. So often."

Navinda sat on the side of the bed. "Come here, Peter."

Peter sat next to her. He held her hand. "I'm sorry."

"Do you think you are alone?"

"No. It's just that I go down to the sea for answers. Sometimes I get them. But I know that's stupid."

"Who is this girl you wrote this poem for?"

Peter hesitated. He turned towards Navinda. Her eyes were shining. "It's for you. I wrote it after I met you in the café. I came home. I dreamt that I walked down to Eastcombe, that you were with me."

"Yes?"

"But you weren't really with me. It made me cry. I thought we'd never meet again."

Navinda clasped Peter's hand. "Sometimes I want to do that too. What you wrote – I want to walk blindly out into the dark and keep walking on and on. I want to walk with you, Peter."

"I think I …"

Navinda placed a slender finger across his lips. "Don't say it. Walls will spring up around us."

"We kissed before, Navinda. In Mrs. Benji's room."

"Yes. Did you think that was wrong?"

"We lay down together," he said. "I was so nervous."

"A girl of my background has to be careful. I should not be here with you. If I touch you, that means so much."

Peter gnawed his lip. "There's something I need to say. If you ever feel you …" He hesitated and looked fearfully at

Navinda. "Erm … don't care for me, don't want …" He forced the words out. "To see me anymore."

"Yes?"

"Promise me you'll tell me. I couldn't bear it otherwise." He looked pleadingly at her.

Navinda smiled and drew him towards her. "If I felt that could ever be the case, I wouldn't be here. As I said, I have to be careful."

"But there must be boys at your school who like you. I imagine there must be hundreds."

Navinda threw her head back. "Ha! Hundreds! What sort of girl do you think I am? Every day I go to school, and these hundreds of boys follow me! Ha!"

"But there must be one."

"Yes. Wahaj. We are friends."

"Friends?"

"Yes. He never tries to woo me. He just thinks I should be with him and that is that. He would never write a poem about me. He would not talk about his real feelings. His fears. About our journey together." She paused. "Not like you do, Peter Young." She looped her arms round his neck. "There is so much to discover with you. But I do not need to waste my time with guesswork." She drew him to her. "I am ready, Peter. Walk me blindly into the dark."

Peter stirred. His left arm enclosed the slender form of Navinda. It seemed miraculous that she was with him, holding him, her body pressed against his. She was sleeping. He felt the imprints of her kisses on his face and lips, her hand warm against his skin, and her breath – the touch of a feather – on his cheek. It was amazing and magical to be chosen. For Navinda to say that, despite all fear and danger, she wanted to be with him. And only him. He didn't know who Wahaj was. Had he and Navinda been together like this? It didn't matter to Peter, and he felt a tremor of sorrow for this boy he had never met, who probably loved Navinda just as much as he did.

For the first time, Peter realised how deep and significant it was, the immensity of the risk for a girl. For all the excitement and desire he felt, he understood the commitment of flesh and blood, body and soul, the gift of eternal love. More precious than the gems of Ind, trembling, beautiful, radiant, shining. And it was a gift he was making too. But, for Navinda, it was a sacrifice. For that, he knew she would be his first thought, his eternal focus, the centre of their love-flame. And he would never neglect it. For without it, there was nothing.

And what would he bring? Liberty of mind and soul. No walls. Their boundaries would be the distant foothills and mountains of reason and hope, and they would climb those too. He would bring his wayward poetry and music to their life mission. He would do it, completely and utterly.

There was a thud. Something had been dropped in the hall above. Footsteps. Someone cursing. "Navinda," he whispered. He kissed her lips and she responded, drawing him onto her. Her eyes half opened. "Somebody's in the hall above." Her body went tense. Peter reached for his T-shirt and pulled on his jeans. Navinda slid from the bed and put on her sweater before buckling on her denims. She laced her black boots and stood up. "The Golden Hand?" she mouthed. Peter shrugged. They crept under the wooden steps that led up to the hall door. Whoever was in the hall was hunting for something. A creak resounded from above. The footsteps moved towards the kitchen. Silence.

"They might come around through the garden," said Peter. "Probably guess we're down here." He reached up and jerked the light cord. "We must be ready." They crept across to the outside door then stood against the wall on either side.

"I'm ready," said Navinda.

I Walked the Beach with You Last Night is from John's novel,
A Game of Chess – Collingwood 2018.

DOCTORS' WOOD

Thomas placed his boot on the lichen-stained granite stone. Page, Hendrix and Clapton had already climbed the steps and now stood on the wall's edge, silhouetted against the blue sky.

"Come on, Daddy Thomas!" said Clapton. Thomas clambered up the steps and stood on the wall. A cart track curved along the edge of the field, and the children ran ahead; Page, in her plaits and yellow hoodie, pursued the burly Hendrix, while little Clapton scampered along gamely behind. It was a morning of startling beauty – azure sky, soft breezes, and a dramatic sun lifting in the east, burning in the dazzling blue, its light refracting on the white farm buildings. The perfect antidote to the darkness Thomas had been experiencing.

He had been in his study, staring dumbfounded at a newspaper. There was a picture of a priest, holding the limp body of a dead child; a terrorist bomb in Beirut had killed the little boy. His small blue shoes looked freshly tied, and his tiny T-shirt and shorts still showed the creases from ironing. But he was dead, and the priest was weeping. Around him was a maelstrom of drifting smoke and collapsed buildings. "Where are you, God?" the priest had cried – this was used as the headline. It was a question Thomas could not answer. Where was God when he was needed? Why had he not plunged from the sky and lifted the child from the inferno with a divine hand? Where *was* God? Thomas shut his eyes and trembled. The children had come into his study with their coats on, ready to go out. Thomas folded the paper and summoned a smile.

The children had struck across the field along the footpath to Doctors' Wood. They had arrived at the stile and sat on the rail, looking back at Thomas. He walked after them before stopping in the middle of the field. The peal of church bells from the neighbouring village rolled up the valley and threaded joyfully through Doctors' Wood, engulfing Thomas with a jubilantly random melody, accompanied by the hushing and swaying of the oaks and birches. Where was God? Thomas looked at the children, who were shading their eyes from the bright sun. Page waved. "Come on, Daddy Thomas."

Where was God? In that instant, Thomas knew God was in him. Whoever had killed that child with a bomb had tried to play God. Whoever had forced that family to flee from their burned home believed he or she had the power of God. Thomas knew his duty would be to die – if he had to – to save his wife and children. And to save others. As many of the multitude as he could save. It didn't matter if they did not believe in his God or believed in any other god; it was his calling to save and protect as many as he could. And there would be other willing hands ready to serve and join in the gathering of the harvest.

Thomas smiled at the realisation that this insight had arrived amid contemplating a vast field of turnips. He did not care. Perhaps a field of dancing sunflowers or gleeful, golden sheaves of corn would have been more appropriate, even biblical. It did not matter. He was not a clever man. He knew that. He knew other people knew. He also knew God was within him, in his hands and fingers, in his eyes and heart and mind. *Of course!*

He walked briskly along the track to the stile and lifted little Clapton into his arms and kissed his grubby forehead.

"Hey, Daddy Thomas," said Hendrix. "You had a moment, man!"

Thomas contemplated Hendrix's brown eyes and dark curly hair. "Yes," he said.

"You was looking at the sun an' the big world turnin'. I saw you."

Thomas stared in wonder at Hendrix. He could be surly. He knew he missed his father.

"You was thinkin', *What's it all for, man? What's it all for?*"

Thomas stood rooted to the spot. He never had suspected Hendrix would speak or think like this.

"And then you knew. Right?"

"Yes, Hendrix." Thomas spoke softly. "Yes. I knew."

Page slipped from the gate and slid her arms around Thomas's too ample waist. "I feel that too," she said. "I look at the sky, and I think about how small I am. Then how big I am."

Thomas drew her to him. "What about you, Clapton?" he said to the little boy's sunny face.

"I don't want to see no zombies, Daddy Thomas."

"You've got your lightsaber. You can protect us!" said Thomas.

They climbed the stile, and Thomas placed Clapton on the path. The boy brandished his lightsaber at a startled hogweed. Hendrix took his hand. "C'mon, little man."

They meandered along the narrow path, stepping over the limbs of fallen trees. Animal tracks and badger holes told of an underground world of tunnels and nests, death and life and decay. Thomas shuddered at the thought. Hendrix had plucked and peeled a wand of hazel and was using it to decapitate nettles and brambles as they cut their way through the brush. Page was singing a song about a 'fat old sun'. The church bells had fallen silent, and Thomas had begun to sense a completeness in his life. It was not to last.

Page screamed and pointed to the ground. "Look! Look!"

"Wow," said Hendrix.

Clapton clutched his brother's legs. "Daddy Thomas! Look!"

On a severed tree trunk, an adder coiled like a whip – striped, black, with steel-grey skin – then lifted its snout head, venom loaded. The split blood-red pupils stared, and its flicker tongue licked the air.

"Wow!" Hendrix repeated. He lowered his head towards the snake.

"Leave it. Don't touch it." Thomas tried to speak calmly as his stomach churned.

The armoured muzzle moved fractionally, its tongue darting, and held the silence; Hendrix saw the sinister black X on its neck and crimson eyes – alien, engineered, waiting. A stick cracked. A writhing and thrash of the whip and the adder shot into a rabbit hole. The children stared in horror at the stump where it had been.

"Wow! Wow!" Hendrix whispered. A whimper came from Clapton as well.

There was a crash in the thicket of saplings and brambles. Thomas turned. Something was stumbling away through the trees. It broke into a run.

"Stay here!" Thomas shouted to the children before dashing towards the coppice. "Hey! Stop!" He saw the brown hoodie and grey jeans of a man scrambling down a slope into a narrow gulley. He tried to follow whoever it was, but the figure had gone. Thomas stood, panting. He stumbled back through the crushed bracken and tumbled tree limbs. As he did, he caught the haunted looks on the children's faces.

"Who was that?" asked Hendrix. Clapton still clung to his legs.

Page stood, innocent and wondering, in a shaft of sunlight. "What's happening, Daddy Thomas?"

Thomas tried to compose himself. "It was nothing."

"It was someone," said Hendrix. "Some dude."

"It has gone. *He* has gone." Thomas tried to smile. "It's fine. You're quite safe here. Safe as houses." But Thomas knew in his heart that they were not. Hendrix had seen something.

From John's novel *A Game of Chess* – Collingwood 2019.

PICKET POST

A young couple, Roland and Dawn, decide to sleep in the New Forest overnight….

Roland had chosen a Phantom 350S for this trip. A sleek black box off-roader. Climate-control, keyless, Bang & Olufsen surround sound, seats of decadent black leather. Dawn said it looked like a high-class hearse. Wearing camouflage print jeans and khaki T-shirt, she flicked her phone as the car cruised, a silent ghost, down the A31, into the slip lane to Ringwood. The police station, a concrete sarcophagus, hove into view and the Phantom swept into the car park.

"Won't be a minute," said Roland and kissed Dawn's soft lips. He stepped on to the tarmac, every inch the smart young lawyer in his sleek grey suit, steel spectacles, and buzzcut hair with *cool* fade. He slipped a grey attaché case under his arm. He had a dirty job to do. It would not take long. Roland was tempted to wear gloves.

"Who do you want to see?" Roland produced a file and the desk sergeant read the name. He grunted and escorted Roland along a bright corridor. "In here." A key turned, and the steel door swung open, flinging light on to the grey bunk bed and a thin plastic chair and simple desk. "Get up! Got a visitor for you." A curly-haired man swung his legs from the bottom bunk. He slunk towards the chair and looked up at Roland. He was clutching a sheet of white paper on which he had daubed a red crucifix. He crumpled it slowly as he stared, his bloodshot eyes full of loathing.

"I'm Messenger." The expression altered to puzzlement. "Roland Messenger." Roland grinned. "Sorry I'm black." The prisoner blinked and shook his head. "From Nyx & Thanatos. Solicitors. You need to sign these papers."

"Oh, right," he mumbled. He stank of sweat. *Probably still high on something*, thought Roland. He slid the document file from the case and opened the folder on the table. "You need to sign that you have seen these. You don't have to read them." Roland felt a smile twitch the corners of his mouth. Had the man noticed? He didn't care. Let this be over. He did not want to share the air.

"Here!" Roland flicked the document pages and jabbed a finger on the bottom line. The prisoner's pale hand hovered. Roland slipped a black fountain pen between his fingers and unsheathed the cap, revealing the platinum nib. Ink globed on the tip and a black blob dropped – a silent bomb – on to the grey desk.

"Sorry," he breathed.

"Just sign," Roland said, and guided his trembling white hand to the line, steadying his thin wrist. "Here." His signature was surprisingly elegant and concluded with a flourish. "Excellent!" Roland flipped the folder shut and slid it into the case. "They'll be in touch." The man managed a wan smile and his eyebrows lifted beneath the mop of hair.

"Thanks," he whispered. But Roland was through the door, heard it slam behind him and the key turning. Freedom!

Dawn was waiting by the car, her lovely face full of light. "Was it OK?"

"Horrible guy. After what he's done … seemed so normal. Easier if he had been a monster."

"Your clothes are in the back."

"Amazing. Can people kill with their normality?"

"Roland. It's done. Let's enjoy this."

"Yes, sorry. Thanks." He looked into her loving eyes.

She smiled. "Better not get changed here."

"True, but I can get rid of this." Roland hurled his suit jacket on to the back seat and pulled off his tie. "That's better!"

"How much are we going to save by not staying in a hotel?"

"Three hundred quid."

"Wow!" The sun glinted on the silver crucifix pendant that he had given Dawn as an engagement present.

"For the wedding pot," he grinned.

They drove from the town and threaded their way through the back lanes. Pigs and sheep poked their snouts through the slits of animal trucks waiting for the farmers' market. They ascended Crow Hill, and the verdant meadows, tousled heaths and narrow glades of the New Forest unfurled as a vivid carpet before them. There was a silent woodland and stream that Dawn would like. Picket Post.

Work for the day being done, Roland reasoned, they would walk the fragrant dells and step across the tumbling streams, watch the white egrets fishing in the shallow waters, and the redshanks combing the tidal mud and wet margins for worms; observe the peregrine falcons, alert and menacing on fence posts and shingle banks, and shimmering dragonflies dancing above the swirls and eddies of tiny creeks, and rivulets that spun blue threads across the turfy fields. They would contemplate the quietly grazing ponies, hind hooves tilted, manes gently lifted by the summer breeze. It was this living vibrant world of intimate colours and natural sounds that would be the landscape for their marriage and mission together.

Roland turned the car on to a rugged stone track; the Phantom bumped and swayed, stirring a dust cloud, before finally turning into a narrow glade, coming to rest under the stooping boughs of an oak tree. They could hear the softly tumbling brook deep within the tree canopy, and they were surrounded by mighty gorses, yellow-flowered, nodding and swaying with giant bell heathers of magenta and pink, humming with nectar-loving insects while, beneath their weighty flower-laden arms, green tiger and stag beetles patiently brought order to the forest floor.

As Dawn laced up her walking boots, Roland buckled up his jeans and pulled a khaki shirt over his head. Equipped with phones, map and sunhats, they plunged joyfully into the forest's kaleidoscopic landscape of pastels, vivid blooms, dancing giant daisies and twittering birds. Crossing the stream on a rickety wooden bridge, they paused to photograph the rare bog orchid, slender swaying cotton grass, myrtle flowers bursting as stars of silver, gold and sapphire, and the crimson carnivorous sundews and butterworts. Fronds of bracken parted to reveal a tumbled group of rocks and flints. The stones lay, an untended grave, at the base of a sprawling yew tree, its leaf laden boughs spread, as in grief or prayer.

* * *

The moon had risen as they wandered back under the stars. They kissed on the little bridge and crept back to the Phantom, as the bechstein bats fluttered and swooped through the twilight.

"The car looks out of place now," Roland said.

"Yes," said Dawn. "An old VW camper is more like us. Why did you choose it?"

"Image." He shrugged. "Doing a job for the firm."

"The suit didn't *suit* you at all," she laughed. "You were playing at being grown up."

"Yes," Roland yawned. "Let's get some sleep."

"Under the stars?" said Dawn.

A shiver of wind shook the surrounding trees, and the moon slipped behind a sudden cloud. "Best not," he said as a salvo of raindrops plunked on the Phantom's gleaming bonnet.

"Got the sleeping bags?"

"In the boot," said Roland.

The back seat folded flat, and they were able to lie side by side in their woolly hats, like two children on their first camp. Daylight deserted the glade. Dawn had perfected the art of sleeping on her front and she pulled a bundle of garments from her rucksack to act as a pillow. She kissed the pendant and slid it beneath the clothes. Her breathing became soft and rhythmic, and Roland knew she was asleep, while he lay staring at the car ceiling. The darkness deepened and became intense. But Roland could hear the restless stirring of the woodland forest and the swaying and nodding of ferns and giant bushes.

He felt himself sliding into a sleep, imagining the footsteps of rodents and badgers and foxes; he pictured them scurrying and scampering among the undergrowth and brush. The moonlight re-emerged and Roland flicked awake. A pony was standing, iron-grey and motionless, its eyes dark and unseeing. The winds shuddered once more, and the pony cantered into the treeline and disappeared.

The gusts were strengthening. Roland could feel a soft tremor as the Phantom shifted and gently rocked. *Sleep*, he murmured to himself and turned on his side, closing his eyes, and pulling the sleeping bag about his head. Had it been such a good idea to plan a sleep-out? They had done it before. Under the dizzying Pacific night sky at Orokawa beach where branches from Pohutukawa trees adorned the white sand, like dinosaur bones, lizards scurried up tree trunks, and dolphins soared like sea-jesters from the waves. Roland smiled at the memory and dozed.

He startled awake and looked at his watch. 3am. Damn! He had to go outside. No choice. He struggled out of the sleeping bag and slid on his boots. He yawned, before opening the door. The storm had risen and all around the car the giant fronds of bracken and gorse shook and thrashed as the winds cut through like an invading army of ghosts. In the moonlight, he watched the bending and bowing of saplings, and the stooping boughs of the oak tree slapped and clawed at the car windshield.

Roland looked about uncertainly. The pony had scared him. He stepped gratefully back into the car, and sat upright behind the driver's seat, his eyes flicking across the shifting images that cavorted around him. But it was the shadowy spaces between the trees that stirred fear. Was he looking at strange forms and creatures of a dark age, a primeval Hades? The jostling of hands and arms and feet and eyes glancing or staring, with gnarled fingers and limbs pointing and waving? He shook his head and tried to focus. Roland felt the eyes of another creature upon him. He pictured the ghostly apparition of a horse, its muzzle and crest brutish, eyes dark and menacing.

"Dawn, Dawn!" Roland shouted "Quickly, love." She jolted awake and seized his arm. Roland dared not look in the rear-view mirror. They heard the straining of a cable as the car rocked and shuddered in the gale. They watched as the handbrake magically lifted and disengaged and the steering wheel rotated under the control of invisible hands. The car began to move. Dawn gasped as the Phantom rolled backwards.

"Dear God! What's happening!" cried Dawn. "We're not wanted, Roland."

Roland leapt into the front seat and fumbled for the keys, as the woodland raged and tossed. The Phantom had moved away from the oak tree into a clearing. Ahead, the moonlight illuminated the dancing madness of the forest. But before their eyes a blackness emerged from its centre, a heart of darkness was stalking towards them, its blank and cold eyes fixed. Roland had seen those eyes before. "There is something here," he breathed. "And it hates us!"

He turned the ignition and the car roared into life, headlights blazing into the pitch dark. Roland wrenched the wheel to the left and the Phantom shot to the end of the track. The engine died. Roland frantically tried to restart the car. They could feel a stygian gloom swarming and enveloping the space about them. Dawn screamed. "Get us out, Roland!" The Phantom awoke, and roared into life, and the car leapt and hurtled along the rugged track in the chaotic howling moonlight, before meeting the road.

And they drove, drove like the wind, eventually meeting the comforting illumination of the motorway and the service station. They held each other, shaking, sitting at the cherry red table in the Costa Cafe, sipping lattes and relishing the anonymity and soullessness of the place.

It was when they walked back to the Phantom that they saw it. A blood red crucifix, daubed on the tailgate, crimson runnels dripping down to the fender. Roland and Dawn stood quivering in the chill lamplight.

They reached home before sunrise. Dawn lit the log fire. As the sticks hissed and flamed, they held each other in the glow. "What did it all mean?" said Roland.

"It was a warning. To both of us. We did not care enough. Perhaps you did not care enough about that man."

"The one at the police station?"

She nodded. "A warning like no other. To be us. Don't surround ourselves with beauty and then think that we are in paradise." Her voice tremored. "Not to think we can do what the hell we like."

Roland nodded slowly. They stared into the flames.

Next day, Roland took the car back to the rental company. "I apologised. It was easier to do that than try to explain. I had to pay for the damage of course."

"How much?" Dawn shivered and looked down.

Roland smiled painfully. "You know how much, Dawn." She turned her face away. Everything had altered.

Sometimes, in a dream, Roland would still see them, before his helpless sight. A grey army of phantoms, lost souls, the unregarded, the barbarian, the unloved, the forsaken, the shamed and brazen, the ragged, running riot like an insane militia among the oaks, slender birches, and ancient yews.

He would keep this vision to himself.

It was too dangerous to set it free.

Picket Post is close to the A31 in Burley, Hampshire. A map of 1675 shows the drawing of a crucifix at this point. 'Picket' is a collective word for a group. In 1894, it was noted that "this once well-known forest tryst … A picket of soldiers was formerly stationed here to suppress the poachers, smugglers, and other lawless folk of olden days".

MONTY AND THE HELL BUNNIES

Monty the cat watches a Goth Band perform at Miss B's fancy dress party

Onty, the village cat, was perched on a dry-stone wall, surveying the extraordinary goings-on at The Fossils – the vast rambling home of the eccentric Miss B. He had chosen his vantage point carefully, as he always did. He was perfectly positioned to intimidate the ostriches, Nora and Dora, who had been shut into a wire pen, the gate carelessly secured with a rope looped over the post. Agitated by the spectacular events at The Fossils, they strutted dementedly around their enclosure, taking it in turns to glare and hiss at Monty and shake their vast wings.

The Hell Bunnies were now warming to their task. "Good evening, Diiiingweeell," shrieked Hell Bunny, the lead singer, sporting a mauve body stocking and giant purple ears. A skeletal Lady Macbeth on keyboards evoked a cacophonous afterlife into which she appeared to have already passed. Gothalips pouted and strutted on bass, while Big Frank (Frank.N.Stein) – under a mane of lustrous, flowing black hair – was testing the limits of an enormous drumkit he looked determined to destroy. The result was a pulsating rhythm that made the golden marquee quiver like a gigantic blancmange.

And so – to the thunderous rhythms of *Who Let the Bats Out* – straw men cavorted with multicoloured peacocks, and grizzly bears with nuns in fishnet tights. Wilfred Plunkett was having a wonderful time: Mustardseed – having imbibed rather too many Wicked Witch Apple Punches – had become detached from Tinkerbell and was performing a frenzied clog dance with a miniskirted Sleeping Beauty – his arms, as he rotated, reaching upward as if to pluck invisible fruit. All thoughts of lumbago and rising blood pressure departed as Wilfred swirled and capered.

Finally, they joined hands and spun, creating an arc that scattered the other partygoers, who whooped and applauded. As Wilfred revolved, his face was a picture of rapture, the years shed, and he was – once again – the dashing young officer from Sandhurst. After the next circuit, he realised he was a little dizzy. Another circuit and he realised he was feeling rather unwell. The apple punches were combining with the Breast of Troll and Sorbet of Leech to devastating effect. The Ogre's Eyeballs that Wilfred had eaten now resembled his own. Sleeping Beauty's expression transformed from happiness to horror as she realised her aged amour was in imminent danger of throwing up. She hastily released her hands, and the old man bolted towards the exit. He burst from the marquee and raced frantically across the garden, where he collapsed onto a wire fence and vomited profusely.

Nora and Dora were not amused. A gaping Wilfred lifted his ashen face only to be confronted by what appeared to be a gigantic turkey, with wings the size of twin umbrellas and a long neck and crumpled facial expression that reminded him of his aged uncle Enoch. The turkey opened its beak and hissed. A bolus of masticated beetles, bat droppings, and fruit shot from its mouth, squirting Wilfred's face and spattering his eyeglasses. Mustardseed squawked and ran for his life. He careered blindly towards the Transylvanian Pond and tripped – decapitating a statue of Dorian Gray – before plunging in headfirst. Two black swans, who had been calmly cruising the dark waters in the twilight, reacted with fury. As Wilfred rose soggily from the water, the furious fowl flapped their wings and chased the old man up the drive, with Tinkerbell in hot pursuit.

By this time, Monty had sensibly taken his leave, deciding that a warm fire and a modest snack, courtesy of Gideon, would be preferable to the bizarre revels at The Fossils. Nora and Dora, however, were not inclined to agree. Having triumphed over the hapless Mustardseed, they charged against their enclosure, trampling down the wire fence before setting off at full speed to join the festivities. The first person to be aware of these uninvited guests was Miss Stamp, the short-sighted village postmistress, dressed as an emu. She suddenly found herself in the company of a very tall, convincingly attired ostrich. Miss Stamp was about to ask her companion if she was new to these parts when Nora suddenly pushed passed her and made a beeline for the banquet. She was joined by Dora and, with incredible speed, the pair devoured the entire spread, slurping down blood-red jellies in one gulp and demolishing the handmade replica of Dracula's castle. Nora then grasped a roasted suckling pig, relieving it of its apple, and sent it flying into the partygoers. The enormous birds then turned their attention to a tureen of plum and pineapple fruit punch before abruptly racing towards the stage.

The Hell Bunnies glanced nervously at each other as the villagers scattered, sending plastic chairs bowling across the dance floor. "Bloody Nora!" shrieked Hell Bunny, as Gothalips dropped her guitar and screamed. Lady Macbeth was, at first, unmoved. "Out, damn spot!" she shouted imperiously. "Screw your courage to the sticking place!" she screeched at the departing Gothalips. But Nora and Dora were approaching at full throttle.

"Oh, bollocks!" Lady Macbeth lifted her multiple skirts, leapt from her stool, and raced for the exit, sprinting the full hundred metres at astonishing speed before hurling herself into the rear of the band's battered Transit. Frank.N.Stein was left to contemplate a solo performance. An audience of two gigantic ostriches, however, did not appeal. He vaulted over the loudspeakers to a tumultuous crash of timpani and bongos. Nora and Dora mounted the podium, hissing at the departing performers, before barging through the rear of the marquee and into the garden, leaving a vast slick of ordure in their wake.

* * *

Loud cheers erupted from the garden at The Fossils. Miss B was being conveyed in a black sedan chair by an unkindness of four scantily clad male ravens – whose black feathers offered a tantalising glimpse of their rippling muscles and prodigious beaks – before she was lowered into the gigantic golden bed. At the foot, two fallen angels unfolded their crow wings. The ravens each moved to a corner of the bed and pulled a lever.

The bed slowly rose into the air, the rope tethers unravelling from their coils. Miss B spread her arms wide, the evening breeze fanning out her grey hair, as the parishioners clapped and shouted. A trumpet voluntary of ram horns rent the air, as clouds of dry ice billowed from beneath the bed. A volley of rockets shot upwards and exploded into a miasma of stars. Spotlights and lasers, mounted on The Fossils' roof and two giant beech trees, compounded the drama as Nora and Dora emerged from behind a massive japonica.

A kick from Nora sent the first raven flying, and the others immediately shed their wings and ran for their lives. Miss B's ecstasy at her graceful elevation into the night sky was short-lived as the ropes uncoiled and the old lady realised she was indeed in for the ride of her life. As the bed rose above the mock-castle walls, a sea breeze sent Miss B on a journey across the village of Dingwell. When she drifted past the church spire, she wondered if that little tab of ecstasy – supplied by her dear grandson, Kevin, hidden under the Strawberry Temptation in a box of Milk Tray – had taken complete possession of her senses. Below, the revellers were gripped by panic while Miss B cruised across the starry firmament.

Dora and Nora had the stage to themselves as the villagers had swarmed up the drive or fled into The Fossils. One group found their way into the murky medieval kitchen. They huddled together as a firework exploded and cast an eerie light through the gothic arched window, dramatically illuminating Roger, the voluble cockatoo. His vibrant plumage vivid in the garish light, Roger strutted Godlike along his lofty perch. His head rotated, its fiery golden crest rising – like an avenging angel about to pronounce hellfire and damnation.

"Dear Lord!" wailed Miss Stamp, squinting through her milk-bottle spectacles. "Have mercy on us!"

Roger's beady eye blinked, black as pitch. Ominously, he stretched his wings. Miss Stamp trembled. The terrified villagers gasped.

"Bollocks!" said Roger.

From *A Game of Chess* – Collingwood 2018.

THE HOLLYWOOD HAIR
SALON

**Graz, Austria – it is 1948, and Eva Bauer awaits
her most important customer….**

Eva Bauer inserted the old metal key into the lock. She
struggled to turn it but eventually the mechanism
rasped, and the green door of Bauer's Hollywood Hair
Salon creaked open. She walked behind the reception stand,
placed her blue trench coat and handbag on the chair, and slid
her canvas suitcase beneath the counter. She flicked on the
light switches. One by one, neon strip lights flickered into life;
with one, a violet core of light would glow and slowly expand
to the length of the tube before casting its light down. The
leather and chrome styling chairs were parked in front of
mirrors, like spectators anticipating the beginning of a drama
or prisoners awaiting interrogation. A cluster of pink-domed
hairdryers on chrome stands stood as a group of aliens, waiting
to be deployed.

Eva flipped more switches. Cabaret globe lamps
blinked into life around the mirrors, casting a white pool on to
each chair. *Perfect*, she thought. Each seat now seemed
prepared for an opulent Austrian officer's wife to sit – lips
puckered in a pose of exquisite boredom – and await the
magical transformation from *stumpf frau* to siren beauty. The
neon lights transformed Eva's otherwise drab premises into a
theatre of dreams for the corpulent men and frustrated wives
of the cultured Austrian city of Graz, with its baroque palaces,
quaint boulevards, and picturesque Gothic cathedral.

Eva cut the string on a bundle of the latest magazines. The glossy covers spilled across the counter as Eva looked admiringly at the images from *Vogue*, *Mademoiselle*, and *Royal*. "1948, the Year for Women!" was the strapline on *Die Dame* magazine. Eva tutted at the cover picture of a young blonde woman in a tedious beige dirndl – a flowing long skirt with a purple corsage and a plain white blouse. The maidservant's floral apron matched the girl's benign and submissive smile. Eva simmered. *A lovely young woman, dressed like an antique!*

Eva was dressed similarly of course. It was expected of single women, but she had dallied with a dramatic waistcoat of magenta velvet and a flowing skirt of darkest crimson. Her mother's platinum brooch added a dash of Art Deco, and the maroon lipstick a libertarian panache. Eva's blonde hair was pinned back but a fringe of curls endowed her blue eyes a darker emphasis and a soupçon of intrigue. Eva shuffled the magazines together and carried them to the black coffee table in front of the mahogany and white velvet sofa. Two glass ashtrays, an eagle-shaped jug and crystal tumblers glittered on the table, and Eva's prize Girmi Moka coffee maker completed the scene.

Eva returned to the shop window and, reaching between the voiles, she rearranged the crystal bottles of exotic fragrances and hair treatments, antique curling tongs, and glittering silver combs and brushes on a carefully folded satin sheet. Smiling portraits of Ava Gardner, Marlena Dietrich and Clark Gable endowed this shimmering tableau with glamour and opulence. Eva loved to create her interior landscapes, enjoying the symmetry of professional purpose and aesthetics. She loved the paintings of Friedrich and the sculptures of Hagenauer. A bronze figurine of a mother and child stood proudly on the sideboard. *What I am about to do, I do for you,* she murmured. The coffee pot was quietly bubbling. All ready!

Today was to be a special day. There was to be only one customer: Herr Maximillian Schmidt – he allowed Eva to call him Max. He wanted no one else to be in the salon. "Not everyone should know about the little things you do for me, madame!" Herr Schmidt had paid for the hairdryers – he claimed they were all destined for American soldiers' wives, but he had the consignment diverted. "How clever I was, Madame Bauer, do you not think?" he had boasted, as she combed black dye into his greying hair. "And the moustache, please madame, I want it just like Mr Gable's!" Eva had snipped and trimmed the moustache perfectly into the thin pencil style so beloved by Austrian men. "Perfect, Madame! I will be the talk of the Rhetorik Club! Ha!"

Today, Eva knew he would want her to shave his back. "I feel like an animal, a brainless ox, a brute! Then when you shave it, you set me free, Madame!"

Eva had not put Herr Schmidt's name in her diary – she had written 'holiday' across the whole page. She returned to the door and reached up to change the sign to OPEN, as she always did. No. Leave it as closed. Herr Schmidt always entered by the back door, preferring to be discreet. Eva pictured his short arrogant gait, his paunch straining the buttons of his Loden jacket - with a traditional stand-up collar that buttoned up to the neck. Furtively, he would open the tall wooden gate into the rear courtyard, and she would see his shadow at the rear window of the salon. She would open the back door as if to a lover. "Fraulein Bauer! What a pleasure!" in his whining voice, as he hung his alpine trilby on a hook and discarded his coat.

But now, Eva was thinking of the railway ticket in her purse. The midday express to Budapest. Her brother would meet her at the station and then a taxi to the Seventh District of the city, and the old Jewish quarter. She trembled at the excitement.

Eva glanced in the mirror behind the reception desk, extending her arm to straighten her hair. As she did so, the sleeve of her lace blouse slid back to reveal a row of numbers tattooed on her slender forearm. Whenever this happened it sent a shock through her, and she would grimace before quickly sliding the sleeve over her arm and buttoning it at the wrist. But now she paused; she caught sight of the white road that snaked over the Graz Highlands to Mauthausen.

Eva closed her eyes and shivered. Herr Schmidt had been an SS officer at the Graz camp, and she recalled him strutting ludicrously, clutching a silver baton, barking orders, gesticulating at the cowering prisoners, averting his eyes and presence from any suffering, turning away as yet another coffin departed through the steel gates.

Had he recognised her? Eva often wondered but did not think so. She turned and opened her special cabinet. She slid open a drawer; a glittering rack of razors, bone-handled, that Eva had polished to perfection, shimmered. A menacing armoury that she would use to shave Herr Schmidt's back. Was this to be the day? She lowered the roller blind on the door. In the absence of natural light, the salon became an intimate cavern, a treasure house of objets d'art, secret trysts, and forbidden conversation. The scene was set.

The ornate Vienna wall clock chimed, and Eva heard the creaking of the gate. Schmidt's chubby face normally appeared at the window. But Eva could see him standing motionless in the courtyard. She opened the door into the rear passage. Schmidt entered, hanging his coat and hat on the usual iron peg. "Herr Schmidt how are you?" said Eva.

Schmidt stared at the floor before casting a troubled glance at Eva. "I did not know whether I should come, Madame," he said slowly. Eva noticed his voice had dropped an octave. His usual irritating bonhomie had departed. "I had a visitor, Madame." He drifted like a ghost to his usual salon chair and sat down, the white light reflecting his suddenly drawn expression. He gazed at the mirror and attempted a smile.

Eva unfolded the grey gown across Schmidt's chest and fastened the stud behind his neck. "Who was this visitor, Max?" She observed the movement in Schmidt's Adam's apple as he stared at the glass.

"It was our parish priest. Huber." Schmidt tried to compose himself.

"Father Huber?"

"Yes, Huber. He was the priest at the camp."

"Liebenau," said Eva. "No one talks about it now." Schmidt looked down. Eva could see his hands fretting beneath the gown. "Tell me. What did the priest say, Max?" said Eva soothingly.

"He said an American officer had come to the church. Huber thought he wanted confession, so they went into the booth. Huber said he refused to give his full name. He said, 'You can call me Captain Raguel', and just sat there in the darkness." Eva began combing Schmidt's hair.

"He said to Huber, 'You were there, weren't you? At the camp. At Liebenau.' Huber said he was, but he was just the camp's priest. Then the American said, 'A friend of yours was there. Schmidt. He was your friend, wasn't he?'"

"And were you there, Max?"

"I was there, Madame. I confess it." Beneath the gown, Schmidt's hands were shaking." I was one of the camp officers. I was there when … when …"

Eva saw tears appear in Schmidt's eyes. "So, what did Huber say, Max?"

"Huber said 'Yes. What of it? All that business had been sorted out. It was in the past. Three years ago.' The American just sat there, in his military cap. Huber could not see his face properly. Just a shadow. Huber asked him if he wanted to confess."

Eva smiled. "Confess? Ha!"

"The American moved his face right up to the grille. Huber could see a scar on his cheek. 'But I have come for you, Huber. Yes, I have come for you'."

"Come for him?"

"Yes. He said, 'Who will speak for you Huber? Who will speak for you?' Something like that."

"What do you think he meant, Max?" Eva's eyes were fixed on Schmidt's reflection, the gaunt, haunted face, the darting eyes.

"Huber asked him to leave, but the American insisted on having my address. Huber had no choice. Now, I confess I am frightened, Eva."

"That the American will come for you?" Eva stood motionless.

"Yes, Eva. I'm terrified. I confess. Terrified each day." Schmidt wept uncontrollably, tears tumbling down his chubby face, eyes rolling and hands wringing in despair.

Eva unbuttoned the gown. "Come. Have your coffee, Max." She grasped Schmidt's hand and led him sobbing across the salon. "You know you always feel calm after your coffee."

"Yes, yes, Eva. You are so kind." He sat on the sofa. "So very good to me." Schmidt's grey eyes blinked as he rubbed away his tears. "I am sorry, madame. So sorry. Sorry for many things."

Eva poured the dark coffee into a china demitasse, placing it on the table with a square of chocolate. "Thank you, Eva. But you are not drinking coffee?"

Eva joined him on the sofa. "You know I love the tea blend at the Sacher Hotel, Max. It is divine." She sipped from a delicate porcelain teacup. The scent of Darjeeling, bergamot oil and cornflower blossoms touched Schmidt's senses. He gazed around the salon and contemplated Friedrich's *The Sublime* – an image of a winter sun between skeletal trees. His eyes moved to the bronze figurine and suddenly felt himself uncouth. "You are so cultured, Madame."

Eva contemplated Max. He had stopped shaking and was now composed. Something of his arrogance had returned and his full lips evolved a smile. She preferred his arrogance, she realised. She watched as he bit the chocolate square, nibbling it like a rodent and coarsely wiping his mouth on his sleeve. "Has the American come for you, Max?"

Schmidt gulped down the coffee and put the cup on the table. "Not yet, Madame. But I found this. A poem or some such. I did not read it properly." He slipped a scrap of paper into Eva's hand. "It had been put under the door of my apartment."

Eva unfolded the paper. She began murmuring the words.

"First, they came for the socialists, and I did not speak out –
    Because I was not a socialist.
    Then they came for the trade unionists, and I did not speak out –
    Because I was not a trade unionist.
    Then they came for the Jews, and I did not speak out –
    Because I was not a Jew.

Then they came for me – and there was no one left to speak for me."

"I am ashamed of myself," said Max. "Ashamed to have cried in front of you, Madame." He smiled sheepishly. *He is craving forgiveness,* Eva observed, *but he regrets nothing.*

Eva refolded the paper. "Max. There is something I need to show you."

"Me, Madame. What can it be? How exciting." His face brightened. "What wonderful surprise do you have for your Max?"

Eva unbuttoned the sleeve of her left arm and drew it back. Schmidt stared at the series of numbers, his eyes startled wide. "I was there, Max," said Eva, suddenly aware of a mounting tidal wave of anger that was turning to a full torrent. "I was there, Max," she cried. "I saw you in your pretty uniform, waving your silver stick, barking like a dog. You were particularly useful, Max, helping to organise the march to Mauthausen!"

Schmidt gaped, his face imbecilic. He shook his head. "No Madame, not possible. How …" he babbled. "How … how?"

"How did I escape? That is what you are wondering, isn't it, Max?" Schmidt nodded. "I was in the kitchen. I hid in the larder. And then in the cellar – with the rats. I heard it all, Max. The shuffling feet, the crying of the women, the praying to God. The boots marching. I heard it all, Max." Her blue eyes pinned Schmidt to his seat. He drew up his knees, foetus-like, and wrapped his arms round his legs.

"I did not know, Madame. I suspected but did not know or guess. There was no hint. And still you knew, and you were happy to cut my hair. And be kind to me?" He looked pleadingly towards her. "I am so …"

"Do not apologise, my dear Max. I prefer it if you did not." Eva would not let him cheat her of her grievance. Schmidt placed his feet on the floor and stared at his shoes. "As you say, Max. It is three years ago. Nobody talks about it now. Or ever will. We must go on, Max. Without regret or guilt. The grass will grow over." She sighed deeply. And Schmidt turned to look at her. "You forgive me?" he said, his eyes full of fear.

Eva smiled. "Drink your coffee, Max. Then come back next week, and I shall turn you into a prince, a consort among men."

"Thank you, Eva. I will see you next Friday. As usual." He gulped his coffee and stood up, patting his mouth with the white napkin. Eva ushered him to the back door. He put on his Loden jacket and Alpine hat and paced across the courtyard. He glanced back before closing the wooden gate.

Eva stood motionless by the back door beneath the glare of the pendant lamp. Time had stopped and she could only sense the fluttering of her heart. The feelings of anger and horror that she had nursed and kindled had now left her, and the ghost of her past was now stalking after Schmidt, an enraged poltergeist that would bring him to his knees.

As if in a trance, she returned to the sofa and picked up the china demitasse and saucer from the table. She wiped the interior of the cup and placed it in a small paper bag. She then put the cup into her embroidered petit point handbag. The paper bag would drop from her hand into the Danube as she stood with her brother on the old bridge. She fastened the bag's buckle, then emitted a sigh. A sigh of weariness, of unburdening, of a solemn vow fulfilled.

The low rumble of a Mercedes taxi jolted Eva from her reverie. It would take her across the Tribeka bridge and the

River Mur – the grey artery that bled down to Liebenau – and on to the Graz Central station.

Eva walked to the counter and put on her trench coat and felt brimmed hat. She adjusted her hair in the mirror and pursed her lips. She flicked off the lights.

The salon fell into darkness. The play was done.

ROARING MEG

Thomas ~ the vicar of Dingwell ~ has a nap in the belfry of his church, to the surprise of his parishioners.

The storm swept up Ayrmer Valley, dragging its grey columns of fierce rain. The wind swept into the belfry and snatched a rope, slamming the clapper against the church bell. Thomas awoke with a start. He gasped in fear and stared as the bell above his head swung. The rope pulled again. The bell tilted and clanged. Then all three bells chimed. Thomas reeled from the cacophony and rolled across the floor.

The trapdoor slammed open. A head – a very shaggy head with a pigtail and bushy eyebrows – poked through, and a face Thomas recognised fixed upon him. "Better stay 'ere, Reverend. Down below is not safe for thee."

A pewter jug of ale and a plate of bread and fruit were slammed on the floor. A traumatised Thomas crawled across to the parapet and stared fearfully over the edge. All Dingwell appeared to have gone mad. A crowd of women and girls chased geese and sheep up the lane and into a field behind his home. An explosion shook the church. Thomas stared in horror as a round shot seared into the roof of his house, setting the thatch ablaze.

He turned and looked down the muddy track towards the Whodhavethoughtit. Men in breeches and doublets were manhandling a large metal vase in a wooden frame into position. The neck of the vase was tilted to point over the pub. This Roaring Meg exploded and fired a huge iron ball, filled with gunpowder. It landed in Doctors' Wood and sent up a column of flame and a shower of earth.

Thomas thought he heard screams, and he saw birds and animals fleeing through trees or soaring into the sky. Other men came running up the lane from the pub and took up position with muskets behind granite boulders and cartwheels. The church bells continued to chime and add to the horrifying scene. Farm workers, with pikes at the ready, amassed at either side of the lane in ambush. The Roaring Meg boomed once again, sending its dark shell arcing over the pub.

Thomas moved his terrified gaze to the west and the length of Dingwell Lane. It was a grisly spectacle. Palls of belching smoke smeared the horizon, and flames leapt from haystacks and cottages. He heard a rush of air, and an iron ball slammed into the wall of Tidy Cottage and exploded. An inferno of orange and crimson burst the doors and windows, and fire consumed its thatched roof in seconds. Thomas watched as a petrified child, her ragged clothes aflame, staggered from the door and collapsed into the lane. All the while, the rattling of muskets had grown in intensity, and he saw the red uniforms of the New Model Army streaming up Yarmer Valley. They swarmed down Martyrs' Lane onto the narrow track outside the pub, where they were met by a volley of musket fire.

Thomas heard the cries and screams above the continuous pealing of the bells. Enough. He must help that child. He lifted the hatch and began the descent down the rickety ladder as the bells continued their deafening ringing above him. The bell ropes danced frenziedly up and down in front of his eyes as he descended. He jumped the last three rungs and landed heavily, crashing clumsily down the stone stairs before bursting through the tiny arched door and into the nave.

Yvonne, Lucinda and Hairy Nigel were clutching their bell ropes as the vicar of Dingwell erupted through the blue curtain that covered the belfry door and slid unceremoniously along the length of a pew, gathering a harvest of hymnbooks as he went, before finally rolling onto the tiled floor.

Thomas staggered to his feet. "I must help that child," he muttered, a haunted look in his eyes. He lurched towards the main door. He hauled it open before stumbling down the church path.

"What's happened?" said Lucinda, stifling a giggle.

"Strange is that!" said Nigel.

"I'll go after him," said Yvonne. "Lucinda, can you pack away, and Nigel lock up?" She headed for the open door. Lucinda followed. "Thomas!" Yvonne called. "Thomas!"

But Thomas wasn't listening. He stood motionless at the kissing gate. He gazed across the lane at Tidy Cottage. It wasn't on fire. Its walls were whole and strong, and Pearl Furkiss was hanging out the washing in her fur coat.

"What you looking at, Reverend? Saucy boy!" she trilled.

Thomas was speechless.

"Thanks, Yvonne," said Lucinda. She looked at Thomas and giggled again before disappearing down the lane.

"Bet you get a bit lonely up in the vicarage on your own. Billy-No-Mates, I calls it," Pearl purred, and opened the side gate. "You can talk to me if you wants to, Reverend. Do you want to?" she gushed.

"Er, no ... I mean, yes," stammered Thomas. "Silly. I thought your house was on ... on ... fire."

Pearl chuckled. "House ain't on fire. But I can tell thee what is." She slunk amply across the lane. "Funny man you are. Needs a woman's touch." She slid her arm round his waist and stroked his nose with her crimson forefinger. "Zat nice?" she crooned.

"She's all yours, Reverend," said Hairy Nigel, bustling past Yvonne and jangling the keys. "That is, if you wants her o' course."

Thomas tried to swallow the lump in his throat, which was the size of a cannonball. "Um, er, bit busy. Got things to ... er ... things to do."

"'Ere you are, Reverend. You take the keys. Marilyn Monroe and I have got work to do at The Fossils. Come on, Pearl. Get yer knickers on. Miss Bonkers will need her dinner. Time for work."

"You isn't no fun, Nigel. And I've 'ad my fill of Miss Bonkers." Pearl Furkiss slopped back across the lane to Tidy Cottage.

"Everything all right, Reverend? Looked a bit shaken up in there. I put the hymnbooks back. No worries."

"Thank you, Nigel. Yes. Had a bit of a fright."

Nigel nodded and followed Pearl.

Thomas leaned against the kissing gate and took a deep breath. Yvonne was standing, blonde and blue-eyed, in her white police running top, tracksuit bottoms and trainers. She was gazing at him; it seemed to Thomas that she knew more about him than even he did.

"You know what you should do with Pearl Furkiss?" she said. Thomas looked puzzled. "Give her a huge kiss, smack her on the bum, and tell her not to be naughty. She'd love it!"

Thomas smiled.

"That's better," said Yvonne. "I don't know what happened to you up there." She glanced up at the tower.

"It's hard to explain … if I can ever explain it. I'm trying not to think about it."

Yvonne moved close to him and clasped his hands. "Thomas …" She looked pleadingly into his eyes. "Thomas, I've been wanting to speak with you … about Alison and me."

"Yvonne, right now I'm no longer sure I'm the right person you need to speak to. But I'll do my best."

"I know you *are* the right person." Yvonne pressed his hands. "You are thinking of resigning, aren't you? I can tell."

Thomas averted his gaze. "I went to the church. I needed to speak to God." Thomas's voice shook. "Stupid."

"And what happened?" Yvonne's eyes were shining.

"I climbed into the church tower. I thought God might be up there."

"And what did you see?"

"I lay down on the floor. And slept. Or at least I think I slept. The whole village went mad. There was a battle. These men brought a gun. A Roaring Meg. It fired over the pub. Houses were on fire. Tidy Cottage was burning, and there was a young girl …" Thomas stood, shaking. "Perhaps I'm going mad." He looked tearfully at Yvonne.

Yvonne touched his arm. Thomas felt a sudden energy flow through him. "You taught us that God's voice speaks in different ways. Perhaps this Roaring Meg was His Voice?"

Thomas mouth opened to frame a reply. But no words came. "I … I …"

"Look at me, Thomas. I am a gay woman. And I need God's guidance. I need him to speak to me. Through you." Yvonne's hands reached for Thomas. She clutched his jacket and looked beseechingly into his eyes.

"If there is love between you and Alison, then be assured that we will find a way." Thomas spoke gently, all the time feeling a new strength flowing into his limbs, a fresh belief in his heart. "Let's talk tomorrow. After work? Come for tea."

Yvonne nodded. "That will be nice."

"All will be well, Yvonne. Be assured of that. And you are full of God's love."

She turned and walked down the lane. Then broke into a jog. Then a run. And was gone. Thomas turned, transformed, towards the vicarage. No longer shaken by what he had seen. He had so much to do.

STOGGIES FARM

A village policewoman confronts an old flame

The beam on Yvonne's head torch danced on the hedges and trees of Church Lane as she sprinted, rhythmically, in the moonlight. A light had been seen at Stoggies Farm. She had to investigate. Now there were no houses. Just bare fields, stark white, stretching back from behind hedges. Oaks and elms cast sprawling, tortured Medusa-like shadows that flowed over her as she ran. Concealment here would be easy, Yvonne thought, recalling the games she had played with Damien as a child: crawling into tiny pockets in lofts and hay barns, or squatting like primates in dark copses or beneath improvised screens of emerald bracken and thorny nettle, or creeping into a mound of straw bales.

On one occasion, she recalled, she had hunted among the tumbled ruins of a deserted cottage, only for Damien to emerge grinning – like an errant Santa Claus – from the chimney breast, trousers and shirt thick with grime and his face smeared with soot. Damien's mother had laughed when Yvonne had presented her son, transformed from mischievous schoolboy to Victorian urchin. As childhood friends, they had been to the same school, sung in the church choir, prayed together, sung carols on the village green by the ancient granite cross. That was in the past. Had he returned?

The time before, she had surveyed his ashen cheeks, and darting eyes, the quivering lips and Yvonne had said no. "No," to his confusion, his bullying, his violence, his chaotic, headshaking bedlam. "No," she had said. "Enough. Goodbye. If you cannot be you, you cannot be with me. I'm sorry." And she had watched him shamble down the lane, in his scruffy jeans, his hair flying and wayward. His backward look, the smile, so charming, so cruel, so blatantly deceptive. A walking lie. And he found lying as easy as breathing. He woke up each morning, looked in the mirror and lied to the same face, casually making a sinner of his memory to credit his own lies. Effortless and natural, his self-myths, his empty, baseless legends. And he was sick. Yvonne knew that. But could not forgive him. His sickness, his stumbling gait, just another ploy.

The road dipped down, and Yvonne swung left onto a disused cart track. She had to pick her way through the debris of old tyres and discarded pieces of machinery. A car chassis sat complete, its axles propped on brick blocks, robbed of its wheels, the steering column comically vertical above the crippled chassis and shattered dashboard. She looked toward the farmhouse. She could see no light. Its peeling front door swung on a rusting hinge, the wooden window frames glassless, their sliding sashes and muntins rotten and flaking. Yvonne stood by the car skeleton. Had someone been here? She looked at the sprouting grasses to the side of the house and shone her torch onto the marks that revealed the depressions and telling shoe prints of a ragged pathway. She followed the tracks, placing her trainers as precisely as she could in the existing imprints.

The track led around to the rear of the farmhouse. The back door had been wedged shut, and a rope hooked the door handle to a nail hammered into the cob wall. Yvonne's heart quickened as she unhooked the cord, and the door creaked open. Her torch followed a series of muddy footprints into the old kitchen. The iron range had long been ripped out, leaving an open fire grate and Spanish basket. Embers glowed, and Yvonne sensed warmth in the damp, fetid air. She stepped into the room. A grimy mattress lay in the corner, and a sleeping bag and soiled sheet were rolled into a bundle. A battered suitcase spilled its contents: jeans, faded T-shirts featuring rock guitar heroes or lists of tour gigs. A plastic bag of grubby underwear and sweaty clothes had been hurled into another corner. Strangely, a single clothes hanger – hooked onto the windowsill – bore a check jacket, clean grey shirt, and striped tie.

The torch beam moved on: a gas ring and kettle, matches, tins of beans, a packet of white bread ripped open. Coffee, a pack of Neptune chocolate bars, a milk carton, a single plate, and a knife and spoon in the cracked sink. Yvonne moved the torch back to the side of the mattress. Beneath a water bottle and a crumpled pack of cigarettes was a newspaper article about a local bands' night and a spilled set of small photographs. Yvonne knelt to get a closer look. These were pictures of happy young children – healthy, smiling, playing. Family snaps of joy amid this scene of filth and human desolation. But who were these people? Yvonne stared hard; she wanted to avoid picking up the photos, leaving any trace of her presence. One was of a little boy with an Afro. Another of a girl with auburn hair and hazel eyes. She took a picture of them. Yvonne didn't recognise these young faces, but she sensed the playing out of some dark, profound tragedy in this Hades of sweat and urine and faeces.

The torch moved again. Yvonne's heart cooled. In the grate, where embers still gleamed, a dirty tray was littered with syringes and needles, used teabags, spoons, pieces of paper, and scissors. More used needles were strewn on a filthy tea towel, with tinfoil, plastic bags, and cigarette lighters. Medication bottles, drink cans, and rags were scattered across the floor.

Yvonne stood up. The torch beam lifted to an open door in the corner of the kitchen. She remembered that door from her childhood. It led to the old lady's privy. She would turn on the single lightbulb and settle down on the mahogany toilet seat, then swing the door shut while she did her business. The old widow of Stoggies Farm used to give the village children sweets and pastries, then retreat behind the door. Yvonne was afraid of that door. Now it was open, and the torch shone into the very heart of darkness. Toilet paper was torn and littered the floor, and Yvonne fancied she could hear the rustling of rodents and spiders. She imagined the stinking toilet-bowl rim alive with larvae, glinting silverfish, and monstrous cockroaches scuttling up from the sewer pipe to feed.

Yvonne bolted from the kitchen and burst into the night. She leaned against the crumbling house wall and exhaled, her breath condensing in the chill air. *Whoever's hiding here will be back. If it is Damien ...* Yvonne shivered. She picked her way back along the track to the lane. She saw the medieval granite crucifix silent in the moonlight on the village green. It was time for a decision. Time to close this chapter.

* * *

Tidy Cottage looked on to the narrow lane that weaved through Dingwell village. Yvonne loved the little back kitchen and snug sitting room and the grey slate flagstones that created a maze-like pattern across her floor. Below them, she knew that an ancient leat ferried water from the watercourse beneath her row of whitewashed cottages and down the valley to the emerald beauty of Ayrmer Cove. To Yvonne, this thread of water was as an artery, a life-giving and cleansing river of renewal that connected her with the slumbering romantic hills and the good earth. When she awoke in the morning, Yvonne could hear the music of the tiny stream and it made her smile as she fed Monty, the feral and opportunist village cat, prior to her morning jog along the quiet lanes and across the fertile fields.

Damien had no such understanding beyond his dissatisfaction with himself. His rivers and tributaries were his arteries and veins in which he sought to inject stimulants that would lift him from his dark self-obsessed reality. Dressed in the ill-fitting jacket and tie, he hesitated before the pastel blue of Yvonne's cottage door, his hand trembling, as he pondered the presence of two women's mountain bikes chained to an iron water pump in the tiny front garden.

Yvonne halted at the corner. A man in a checked jacket was standing in her front garden, raising his hand to pull the cord on her brass ship's doorbell. The mechanism nodded and the bell tinkled.

"Yes?" said Yvonne. "What do you want, Damien?"

Damien turned abruptly, the curls of dark hair framing his brittle face, dark eyebrows, and anxious smile. "Hello, babe. Pleased to see me?" he mumbled. He looked at Yvonne in her white police top and blue shorts. Blonde and beautiful as always. What on earth had he thrown away.

"I don't know," said Yvonne. "In all honesty, Damien, I don't know. It's been a long time. You have a partner. You have children. What has happened?"

"You been through my stuff?" he barked.

"One of the neighbours had seen a light at Stoggies Farm. I investigated. It's my job."

"So, you saw everything. Poked your nose in. I never had no secrets with you."

"Why would you want secrets, Damien? That was your problem. I saw everything."

Damien averted his eyes. "Did you find the … gear?"

"Yes. What's happened to you, Damien?"

He leaned on the wooden gatepost and shook his head. "Oh, stuff. Shit happens you know. Came back, hoping … hoping we might, you know."

"Is that why you're wearing that jacket and tie. They don't match."

"Thought I'd try to … impress." He laughed uneasily. "Can we go inside?"

Yvonne looked steadily at Damien. He was sweating. His lip trembled. Eyes darting. "The last time you were in my house, Damien, you hit me. You cut my lip."

Damien's eyes flickered. "Are you with someone?" he blurted.

"Not a glimmer of shame. I doubt if you even remember. You want me to rescue you. It will be the same. Give nothing. Do nothing. Excuses. Lies." Yvonne's blue eyes were unblinking. "No, thanks."

Damien shifted uncomfortably. He looked at the bikes. "Are you with someone?"

"Possibly. Someone who doesn't hit me. What's it to you?"

"It's just that I thought. If I said I was sorry. If I could … could … change, you might …"

"You were such a star. Had it all. Wrote poetry. Played the guitar. All the girls trailed after you. And you fed on that. Gobbled it up like some schoolboy, and then believed in the myth it all created about you. And you still believe it. You're not interested in anyone else, Damien. You stand in front of a mirror each day and lie about what you see."

The blue cottage door opened, revealing an elegant woman dressed in a purple top and blue jeans. "Hello. I'm Ali. Who's your friend, Yvonne?"

Damien stared. "Sorry. No, I'm just off. I came to see … Sorry. Sorry." He turned abruptly and marched through the gate, giving a last glance towards Yvonne. He walked quickly along the lane and turned the corner. He saw a group of schoolchildren waiting on the tiny village green in the shelter. Some were sitting on the bench in their blue blazers waiting for the school bus, amid a jumble of satchels, hockey sticks and cricket bats. One tiny child was dwarfed by a cello case. They saw Damien. One child said something. They all laughed. Damien shuddered and turned the corner into Church Lane. He leaned against the old stone wall and raised his gaze to the cheerful spring sky. The churchyard's chestnut trees were in full leaf and nodded and swayed their boughs above his head, alternately revealing and hiding the sun.

Damien could still hear the children at the bus stop and was suddenly weary of his life. He wanted to be loved. Have a laugh and a joke. Join in. So, Yvonne had a partner. She was gay. *Still. It settles things. Makes it clear.* Damien felt suddenly, strangely transformed and liberated. Perhaps the fact of Yvonne's identity had opened a door that would enable him to find his own. Yes, it would be without Yvonne. It had to be. He knew that now. And it was a relief and a release.

The school bus roared down the lane and screeched to a halt by the green. He watched the children scramble on board. The bus droned past. One little girl poked her tongue out. Damien smiled. It was what he would have done.

He walked back to the green and pulled the tie from his neck, before placing it into the litter bin. He contemplated the lichen-stained granite crucifix that loomed in solemn judgment next to the bus shelter. Damien removed his checked jacket and slipped it on to the strange obelisk. It now looked comical.

Damien sniffed the scented air and turned back into Church Lane. He would go back to Stoggies Farm and collect his stuff. Then be gone. It would be a walk, he decided, that would take him away from himself. It would be a walk that would not end.

JOHN SIMES

STARGAZY PIE

Don't forget to polish the oji, Zak." Elaine Flaherty looked up from her computer. "We don't want to upset the Iroko man!" Elaine smiled and turned back to her thesis. Jerry was in the greenhouse.

"OK, Mum." Zak sighed and wandered through the kitchen into the garden, plucking the can of cumaru oil and a rag from the shelf. The waves in the bay plashed gently as Zak mounted the steps on to the lawn. The crimson block of oji wood glimmered in the afternoon sun on its granite plinth. Zak knelt beside it. If he really stretched his arms, he could just reach the furthest edge. Zak lay his head on the surface and imbibed the sweet scent of cinnamon and saffron, and marvelled at the textured architecture of the grain. He breathed deeply and eased his body on to the plane, his arms gripping the ends of the slab. Could he feel movement, a perceptible breathing and motion within the sacred tree, the soft beating of a pulse?

Zak turned his head and squinted up at the sun. He closed his eyes again and lay, arms and legs akimbo, feeling the planet's slow turn and rotation, and sensing the new moon travelling as a satellite in the constellation, and the stirring of animals and insects and birds around him. The eclipse. It was happening, shifting, moving. Zak could sense his body stretching and growing and regenerating. How come he knew this but no one else seemed to? Izzy knew. That's why she Instagrammed him. She knew and wanted to be with him. Zak listened to the ocean, bathed in light, feeling the energy on his hands and face. It was time.

* * *

Zak had persuaded his reluctant father to rescue the square slab of iroko oji from the sea. Its dense flesh was blood red. As they were dragging it from the water and the waves

102

crashed about them, Zak felt the sea surge and thunder of the African shore. The wood block – big as a treasure chest – was hauled back to their modest seaside bungalow by a tractor. Dad had mounted it on a granite slab and gave it pride of place in the garden. One of Zak's chores was to stroke cumaru oil into its smooth surface; he could see his reflection in the sheen. On one side, there were several long slits in the wood skin.

"Dad," said Zak, as his father slumped into the armchair feeling his back. "Can I keep it in my room?"

Jerry grinned painfully and shook his head. "That wood is centuries old. People used to believe there's a spirit in the tree. It's a good spirit, but you must not look it in the face." He winked at Elaine. "So, we'll keep it in the garden."

Jerry and Elaine worried about Zak. "Don't you want to play football with the village lads, Zak?" Or "Alice is having a sleepover. You like her, don't you?" And Zak would pull a face and take a reluctant Dixey – the family's somnolent black Labrador – for yet another walk. "He's seeing too much of Miss B," said Elaine.

"Oh, she's harmless," said Jerry. "Just a bit eccentric, that's all."

"Eccentric! She's as mad as..." Elaine paused. "Playing Wagner all day, and those weird paintings of ghosts and spooks and angels and stuff. She keeps talking to him about magic and the stars and all that rubbish. And Zak just laps it up!"

Jerry sighed. "Well, she is your aunt."

"I just wish he'd join in, that's all. He's ten years old. Do what other boys do."

"Look, Zak has a world in his head he likes exploring. And he loves music. And he misses Izzy."

"That can't be helped. Why don't you take him to watch some football? Or rugby. Go to a match?"

"I've tried that. He kept asking me when it was going to finish, and why they were all wearing stupid shorts. Mind you, he did scoff a Big Beast Double Cheeseburger with fries on the way back."

"Miss Prism, his tutor, is worried about him. Doesn't go in the playground. She says he sits on his own and reads or sketches all day. He can't – or won't – do maths. Just draws and writes mad stories. Other kids think he's weird." Elaine turned and faced Jerry. "I think there's something wrong. He's got As … Asp … that thing."

"Asperger's. Look. He's different."

"Where is he now?"

"Out with Dixey, I think. Poor old dog."

"He took his phone and that leftover sausage."

Jerry smiled. "Did he indeed. Well, I don't rate Dixey's chances of getting the sausage. Look. I'll go and find him."

"I'll come with you, said Elaine. "We've got to get this sorted. Where will he have gone?"

"That's easy. Mount Folly. He said today would be an eclipse and full moon at twilight. He's probably up there doing a howling duet with Dixey."

* * *

The tide had retreated so far out. As Zak slowly ascended Mount Folly, each time he turned to look, the ocean – kissed by the sun's western fire – had drawn back further as if in awe of the emerald coast. The shoreline was left stripped bare, sand sucked out to sea, and the beach festooned with rocks and, Zak imagined, debris from sunken ships.

At daybreak, Zak had roused Dixey and they had explored below the beachline; he had peered down through the sliding wavelets and glimpsed ancient timbers, embedded in the seafloor, and dark beds of peat that underlay the old marshland. Now as twilight descended, he and Dixey climbed the grassy track that ran along the edge of the vast fields that swept up to the crest of the mount.

Evening mists formed above the Avon river; a full moon, ghost-white, slid into the eastern sky. As he walked, Zak clutched the silver sun and moon Zodiac pendant – a gift from Miss B, Zak's cheerfully eccentric aunt. He held it up to catch the sun's dying rays.

For Zak, this vivid day had brought an energy and excitement for change that he could see around him but seemed invisible to his bewildered parents. Jerry and Elaine would stare fondly at his freckled animated schoolboy face over breakfast, and wonder at his collections of coloured glass, exotic stones and pebbles harvested from the beach that he would arrange in bewildering rows and patterns. Some he would give names to. Or he would come stumbling up from the seashore, dragging a gnarled tree-branch, and sit cross-legged in the garden talking with the silent timber about how it floated from the heart of darkest Africa, or fallen from a whaling ship, or had been lifted by a storm into the sky before plunging like an arrow into the depths of the ocean.

Zak knew his mum and dad fretted about him not liking football. Enjoying his own company. What was wrong with that? It wasn't normal. And other kids didn't get it. Only Izzy got it. And she wasn't here. Yet she was. Izzy had gone to a place far away, and she had taken with her a portion of Zak's young heart. He looked at his phone again. That same cheeky grin and smile, the flick of blonde hair. Was this 'love'? Was this what it was all about?

But love meant you had to live with someone for ever. Zak doubted he could do that with Izzy. Anyway, she liked horses. She watched that soppy programme *Heavenland,* about girls and ponies and boys, with that deep-voiced American dad with a droopy moustache, and that dim granny baking cookies all day, and barmy panting wolfhounds with cowboy hats.

Izzy's mischievous face and blonde curls peered up from Zak's phone as he walked. He sighed, dragging down his woolly hat over his ears as the chill north wind cut across the fields. On, on he walked, past the long dry-stone wall that traversed the hillside, as Dixey loped and sniffed among the lines of turnips; there were hundreds – purple orbs topped by nodding clusters of leafy stems, quivering, and swaying like the disorderly tresses of ragdolls. Zak half closed his eyes and saw the pleading multitude, the mad waving and trembling of limbs and hands, all reaching skyward. So many. So many.

Zak always wondered how it would be possible for all these crops to be gathered. And yet he saw it every year. He had watched as one of the farm workers bent low and sliced a knife under a turnip. He then stood upright in the sun, chopping the leaf stalks, and nicking the side shoots from the purple globe. He had turned to Zak and said, "That's a good'un. You 'ave it, sunshine!"

The field swept on and up. Zak raised his eyes against the wind. There was a wide gap in the hedge, and it drew Zak's stare to the next field and beyond. On and on, the nodding lines of crops. Incredible. Life rising from the earth. He turned back to the island. That too seemed to be drifting, sliding imperceptibly from the land, as a spacecraft undocking from the mothership.

Zak strode on towards the hill's summit. A muddy farm track veered through an open gate. Finger posts marked an intersection of footpaths and bridleways. Zak imagined himself at the top of the world, having to choose between these ragged routes or to float weightlessly into the sapphire-starred canopy of space. He knew instinctively, there would be a time to do that. But not now.

He was pondering the choice of routes when his phone pinged, and Izzy's smiling face appeared on the screen. Zak flipped open the video message.

"How are yer, lazy dude!" said Izzy beaming. "What yer doing, daft boy?"

"Hi Izzy," Zak gasped. "I'm standing on Mount Folly."

"Cool," grinned Izzy. "I gotta go to school, but I ain't gonna. I got a much better idea, bro' Zak. Let's dance like we used ta!"

"Dance?" said Zak, as Izzy turned her phone towards the TV. He saw her hand reach for the volume control. "Hey, let's get down to these dudes. C'mon." A rock band was at full throttle, the guitarist's flowing locks bobbing to the licks and riffs as the drummer laced and thrashed the drumkit. "Tsh, tsh, tsh, boom, boom, funf, friggin' boom!" shouted Izzy into the phone. "Rock it Zak, and we don't care. Let me see yer!"

"Erm, yeah … erm!" Zak looked about him uncertainly and was rewarded only by a baffled look from Dixey.

"C'mon Zak, you don't dance, you don't love me, and you don't really give a shit! Boom! Boom! Get that dumb dog to shake his hairy ass with these dudes. "Boompf! Boompf! Tish, Tish, Tish, Rock! It!"

And Zak suddenly felt his hips snaking, his shoulders gyrate. He mounted the phone on the gatepost as Izzy's laughing face rotated across the screen. "C'mon, Zak! Tush, tush! Boompf! Boompf. Boompf! Boompf!"

Dixey wasn't the most exciting dancing partner, but Zak grabbed his front paws, and they managed a turn or two, as Dixey tottered on his hind legs and barked. But Zak had suddenly gone full Jackson, Astaire, Swayze with a soupçon of Ninja. *Boom*, Zak drop-kicked a fencepost, rattling the barbed wire; a flock of Marino sheep instantly scattered. "Say it, Zak!" As Zak swooped and swirled and whirled, high kicking the footpath post that shivered and promptly shed some of its digits. "Say it, say it, Zak!"

By now, Zak had gone full Madonna and was sliding his back up and down the wooden paling, as Izzy urged him on. Finally, he stood in front of the phone and rocked for all he was worth. For him, Izzy was audience enough as he pranced and paraded and sashayed and posed and snarled and postured and thrust and strutted his goddam stuff. Even Dixey rose to the occasion, barking and cavorting chaotically.

* * *

Jerry and Elaine peeped fearfully above the dry-stone wall.

"That's our son out there," said Elaine. "With a hornet's nest in his pants."

"And he doesn't give a flying fig apparently!" Jerry grinned at Elaine.

"Up here, hopefully, nobody else does."

"The sheep weren't impressed. Perhaps we should take a leaf out of his book?"

"What? Not give a flying fig either?"

"Come on. Let's get back. Don't want him to see us." They scuttled back across the field and disappeared through the gate.

* * *

Zak wandered disconsolately from the field past the dry-stone wall, through the swing gate and gazed out over the bay. The receding tide had drained his energy and spirit and left him feeling empty and abandoned. Without Izzy, he felt completely alone; a terrible and frightening space remained within his heart. The last embers of the sunset lay like a rim of fire on the horizon. The Eddystone lighthouse blinked. Zak felt the urge to go, to run, to disappear among the flowing limbs of these gentle enfolding hills and valleys. To be gone. To discover a place that was the centre of himself. His world made flesh. That cottage of the soul where he could be truly who he was and not trouble or frustrate or bewilder anyone.

He returned to the warm glow of light from his home. Smoke spiralled up from the chimney in the moonlight, and the vegetable patch lay still and white, dad's garden fork plunged upright in the soil among the innocent winter brassicas and artichokes. Two bean sticks had been tied together in a cross and leaned at a drunken angle. Zak thought of his Tarot pack and the Hanged Man. But there was home. The backdoor opened, flinging a shaft of light across the grass. Mum was standing motionless. "Are you there, Zak?"

"Yes, Mum." Zak walked down the path.

Dixey scampered through the back door, gulped from his bowl, and flopped in his bed, Zak hung up his coat and hat and slipped off his boots and walked through to the kitchen. Mum and dad were sitting at the simple wooden table – she had laid the purple and gold tablecloth that Zak had made for her birthday. Zak's dad lit the tealights and dimmed the pendant. "Dad's made your favourite, Zak." The odour of bacon, eggs and mustard was already warming him. Jerry bent down to open the oven.

"We know this is a special day, Zak." Cradling the terracotta pie dish as an infant, he placed it in the centre of the table on a wooden mat. "We thought you'd like this," he beamed. The heads of sardines poked through the golden piecrust.

"Stargazy pie! Wow! Thanks, Dad." Zak wrapped his arms round his father and clung to him. Mum joined them and hugged each other. Zak sobbed gently. "Thank you, so much. I love you."

"No," said Mum. "Thank you, Zak."

"Yes, Zak," said Dad. "We get it now. We get everything." They held each other, as saplings clinging together in a breeze, swaying gently.

If anyone had passed the Flaherty's bungalow that evening, they may have noticed the boom-boom of rock music, the much-amplified voice of a young girl and swirl of disco lights through the beige curtains.

And yes.

Dixey was dancing.

HURRICANE TARANIS

Zak makes a discovery

Can I go out, Mum? Dixey needs his walk." Elaine Flaherty looked down at her freckle-faced son. She grasped her greying hair into a ponytail and slipped it through a raffia barrette. A storm had been forecast and she could hear the winds gusting and sweeping past the seaside cottage. But Zak was excited. He had been staring out of the window all morning.

"Oh, go on then. But not for long!"

"Cheers, Mum. C'mon Dix!" Dixey, the family's somnolent black labrador climbed reluctantly from his bed and followed Zak through the kitchen. Zak pulled on his parka and boots, tugging his red woolly hat over his fair hair. Elaine watched as they scampered down the cliff path to the beach. Jerry hurried in from the greenhouse and placed a rattan trug on the table; crimson-veined beetroot leaves sprawled among vivid chards and turnip globes.

"How's the greenhouse?" said Elaine.

"Shimmying and a-shakin'," said Jerry. "More of these gales and it will be doing the hokey-cokey. We've lost two panes already."

"It was only a cheap one," she said ruefully. Elaine turned to look through the lounge window at the quivering structure.

"Now you know what St. Vitus Dance looks like," said Jerry grimly.

"Have you ever had to treat anyone for that?" said Elaine.

"Not that I can recall. Mind you, would some even know they'd got it? Round here, people think herpes is a Greek Island."

"What are those white spears that keep flying up the garden?"

"Oh, those. Plumes from the pampas grass. Or at least it *was* pampas grass. It now looks like Zak with a bad haircut."

"Zak's out with Dixey. He wants to look at the storm."

"I bet Dixey doesn't. Poor old dog."

"Zak's been gazing out the window. He's upset. He lost his Zodiac pendant on Mount Folly."

Jerry grimaced. "We can get him another."

"It was from Miss B," said Elaine. "He treasured it." Elaine looked at the graphs and maps strewn across the kitchen table. "He's got his astrology charts out, as well."

"Hurricane Taranis," said Jerry. "Going to be a bad storm."

* * *

Zak was standing in the middle of the beach. The tide was out, but the winds had whipped the waves into creating a glistening sheen of water across the sands, and clumps of foam – plucked from wavetops – hurtled inland, lathering the granite cliff face a dirty white, and plastering a bewildered Dixey - the dog's fur was pasted to him. Zak threw his tennis ball. The wind snatched it, sending it spiralling upwards and soaring over the beach front into the caravan site cowering behind.

Zak squinted toward the sea, enjoying the sheer theatre of the storm, the riotous mountainous waves, the constant movement of light and dark, and the mad cacophonous howling of the winds. A shifting grey mass had obliterated the horizon and was prowling steadily landward, a shrieking poltergeist, peppering rain darts on the shifting ocean. Zak heard a shout. Dad was standing on the beach steps and waving. Dixey needed no second invitation and streaked across the wet sand, ears flying, and scampered up the cliff path for home, as Zak joined his father.

"This really is a hurricane, Zak. Let's get home while we still have a roof on the house."

* * *

Zak approached the silent rock spines that lay, like a dinosaur's back, between the sandy beach and the stony, tumbled chaos of Fairyland. He had been watching the storm's dramatic arrival, the huge tide-surge that injected itself into the tiny valley stream and flowed inland, strewing the beach road with timber and debris, and swamping the hapless caravans; the giant green rubbish skip had been floated, and it bobbed and swirled like a child's toy, crashing into the sea wall. Huge billows had thrown themselves upon the beachfront houses, lifting tiles in layers from rooftops and snatching pleasure boats from trailers, hurling them against granite rocks. Wave upon wave relentlessly pounded the shore, punching holes in the seawall. As concrete blocks tumbled, seawater crashed through, swamping the neat gardens behind.

Zak pondered the chaos unfolding before him. The newspapers and TV were always on about wars and plagues. Were we always on the edge of disaster? Had it been different? Or was there, as the vicar had said, another higher world where it was different? Calm, serene, full of light. And Izzy. Would it be calm and quiet if Izzy were there? Perhaps she wouldn't be allowed in! But if Izzy weren't there, would Zak enjoy it? No, he decided. He wanted something else. There had to be another way.

Now, in the surreal post-storm calm and bright sun, he gazed at the remains of the timber piles from the old quay that used to jut out into the bay, waiting for smoke-belching little ships to bring limestone and coal. Horses would swish their tails as creaking carts were loaded before slowly climbing the narrow lanes. That was an age ago, Mum said. But was it an age? Why wasn't it yesterday? Or last week? What was time anyway?

He turned back to the rocks and picked out the narrow channel that he had used before. It was flooded but some stones had tumbled into it. This time it would not be so easy. Grasping the wet stone ridges, he giant-stepped between fallen boulders, before emerging into a dry gravel channel. As Zak turned, he sensed the presence of another creature. The yellow eyes of a red dog fox held him, ears black-tipped, elongated body and brown legs sprung-poised, a seabass slumped in its jaws. In the instant that Zak had been held in the animal's gaze, it had gone, its brush adding a cavalier flourish of contempt to its departure. The fox scrambled up the shale face to the cliff path and was gone.

Zak stared where the fox had stood, before striding along another glistening channel, the fissure cutting a path between jagged rock spines. He leapt across a black rockpool – deep as time itself – and clambered along a bank of sucking gravel. A granite wall now faced him. Zak knew this was the final barrier. The task was to climb the face while locating his fingers into crevices, before inelegantly hurling himself over the crest on to a shingle bank. Zak looked up towards the summit of the cliff, a hangman's grit of sandstones and shale, blasted loose by the winds, had bled stones and shillet in a long gash down the face; the slate and schist was held in place above Zak by a granite outcrop. Zak clambered up the grey wall and slithered over the rim in a cascade of stones. He hurriedly capered through another channel before emerging on to the white beach.

This was the place Zak felt more excited than any other place. The grey wreckers channel – cut in the ancient stone bed – funnelled inwards to the shore. Zak knew that many ships had been lured to this deadly snare of rock and crag; the smugglers had then looted the ships and murdered those aboard who could not escape. Ahead, across the mass of grey and white limestone shingle lay the flat giant slate of Magic

Rock. Izzy and Zak had made a precious vow to worship the silent stone and keep it as their secret, their place. Izzy said that if she ever wanted to marry Zak – which she might one Tuesday afternoon – they would have to come to this place.

Zak's eyes travelled along the shoreline. Between two rocky outcrops, the storm had gouged out a mass of sandstone and boulders; the giant waves had also crashed into the cliff face which had collapsed and scattered giant stones and gravel. Zak walked to the space between the outcrops. A gully had been gashed at the base of the cliff. Zak scrambled up the mound of loose rocks and peered into the gully. The sea had scoured out a tunnel entrance. Zak held his breath.

An oak lintel, washed white, spanned the square ingress. Gnarled timber planks lined the entrance walls. Zak pulled out his phone. The camera zoomed into the dark doorway. Zak wanted to get closer, but feared the loose pointed rocks and shale perched precariously above the lintel. His foot slid down the shingle and Zak decided to lie horizontal and adjust the focus of his phone. There was a burst of music. "Taraaaah!" And Izzy's cheeky face with the same blonde curls filled the screen.

"What yer doin' in Fairyland, crazy boy. Been dreaming again? Hope you haven't been to our rock without me!"

"No, I …. there's been a storm," said Zak.

"Yeah, yeah, boy, and the cliff crashed, and you found the shaft," said Izzy.

"How did you …?"

"That's because I'm here."

"Where?"

A shadow had appeared on the white shingle. Zak looked at the shadow. It was Izzy's shape. "I'm here, crazy boy! Look at me, dude!"

Zak squinted sideways into the sun. Izzy was standing, in that defiant way she always did. Hands on hips, in her purple leggings and denim jacket and silly pink bows that were much too big. And that soft smile that seemed as wide as the horizon, and light from her eyes as brilliant as the day. "See me now!"

Zak staggered to his feet. He was shaking. His arms reached out and clung Izzy to him, like a rag doll. It was her. That same smell of candy and Ariana Grande perfume that always made him sneeze. "Oh, Izzy. Don't go again."

"I got to, dumb boy. For now. But I'm coming back."

Zak stood up. His nose twitched, and he sneezed. "You're coming b …." and he sneezed again.

"Hey, Zak. I got something of yours. You dropped this. On the hill." She reached into her leather bag. The Zodiac pendant glittered in her palm. "Here. Careless dude. Miss B loves ya as much as me. But I gotta go."

"How …? Go?" Zak was wide-eyed.

"Get in touch with your roots, Zak Flaherty. Irish kin. Taranis storm. Didn't you guess? The storm came for you."

"For me?"

"It was a reminder. This isn't heaven. Wakey-wakey, Zak."

"Look, stop. Stop this. Don't go!"

"Listen crazy boy! People are asking too much of you."

"People?"

"Know yourself, Zak. If the price of finding your place in the world is to lose the world in yourself?" Zak nodded. "Then it's a price more than anyone can faffing afford. Right Zak?"

Zak stood dumbfounded. Tears pricked his eyes.

"You gonna face it?" She placed the Gemini pendant in his trembling hand. The images of the twins glittered. "You could always not give a flying fig. Which is cool!" When Zak raised his eyes again, he was staring at the space Izzy had occupied. He stood motionless. His heart had fled leaving a space inside.

Then Zak ran. He darted across the shingle, vaulted over the granite wall, splashed his way through the channels, bounded down the rocks and emerged on to the beach. He ran straight into his father's arms.

"The storm came for me, dad."

"No, Zak." He held his quivering son.

"It wanted me!"

"But it didn't get you. You're on the good earth, son. Dixey and I were worried."

"Sorry, Dixey." He ruffled Dixey's ears.

Dad kissed his head and smiled down at him. "By the way. Izzy's coming to stay. Her mum phoned."

Zak wondered whether to say he knew. Best not.

"Izzy says you can't manage without her. Dunno what she means."

But Zak knew.

MISS B'S CURIOUS VISITOR

Miss B receives visitors at *The Fossils*

To anyone visiting Twitten Towers Care Home – a neo-Gothic monstrosity which visitors cheerfully renamed The Fossils – an encounter with Miss B could be an unnerving glimpse into the future. Mason, the corpulent grandson of one of the other inmates – as Miss B called them – paused in the act of eating his Big Beast Triple Cheeseburger and stared at a woman who appeared to have already entered the afterlife. She sat on a wooden throne, and clearly intended to spend her unlimited future as Queen of the Space Fairies. Virtually motionless, the old lady's grey eyes were focused on the joyful wooded landscape visible through the gothic arched windows of the old house.

Adding to Mason's sense of the technologically surreal, above Miss B's seat a plasma screen blinked and flashed. Figures of dwarves and demons, fairies and armies, trees striding across a deserted landscape would appear, a continuous video of creatures and monsters and gigantic birds, all moving in sync with Miss B's occasional nod and twitch of her head, or the movements of her lips in wordless dialogue with whatever was making these shapes appear. He noticed that Miss B's right hand, grasping a Pixel Witch wand, would dart and sweep across the shimmering surface of a Demon ePad.

Mason did not know, of course, that this Queen of the Space Fairies had only the capacity to move her right hand and the muscles of her face but was incapable of speech. And yet, this enforced solitude had liberated an inner voice in Miss B that had been suppressed since childhood; now, in harness with technology, the old lady was able to speak and give shape

117

to her inner visions with a clarity that rendered normal discourse unnecessary.

Mason could only gape uncomprehendingly, and he wiped his hands and mouth on his Tranmere Rovers Goth hoodie; his eyes blinked from the depths of the dark cowl, blissfully unaware that he cut the image of a pantomime Grim Reaper. Mason, not unsympathetically, considered Miss B's features and dimly wondered what level of consciousness could possibly exist within this emaciated alien with limbs of chalk, deathly white complexion, a mane of silver streaming from her crown, topped by a platinum coronet of daisies.

She reminded him of a creature from *Alien Exorcism* – Mason had acquired the status of Supreme Phantom in the computer game, having exterminated an entire fleet of death-fighters with his galactic laser – all piloted by extra-terrestrials who shared Miss B's otherworldly features. He stared once again. What sort of bleedin' life was that? No gogglebox. No football. No beer. Perhaps she ate lizards for breakfast – and were those specks of blood around the thin ashen lips? A shout came from across the room. "Mason! Stop starin'!"

Pearl Furkiss, amply filling her blue carer's tunic, bustled into the room as Mason turned his attention to his benignly beaming grandmother.

Miss B had just finished her lunch, and Pearl wiped away the last residues of jam roly-poly from around her mouth. "There you are my love."

Miss B reached for her ePad and scribbled one word: "Lipstick!"

"Oh, right you are. Now where d'you keep your lippy?" Pearl held up Miss B's vast leather handbag. Miss B nodded. "In 'ere? Oh, my Lor'… There's so much stuff in 'ere."

While Pearl rummaged, Miss B looked through the arched Gothic windows of The Fossils. They afforded a clear view of the old cart track as it curved through the grounds beneath the stately oaks and elder trees, and across to the little wood that bordered Stoggies Farm. She had the same view every day. She liked it. She enjoyed the way the winds swung aside the full-leafed branches of the trees to unveil a fleeting vision of the valley down to Wystcombe. *Will the young couple come to the woods again today?* she wondered.

Pearl had found the lipstick and did her best to apply it while Miss B puckered and pouted. In her youth Miss B had scandalised her prim, wealthy parents by appearing topless in *The Daily Splash*—the stable lad had handed a copy of it to her father, she recalled with a smirk. The old man nearly swallowed his pipe. Her next outrage was to be photographed again – which she had arranged – dancing naked at the Isle of Dogs Pop Festival with her completely stoned friends, her body painted purple but for a single sunflower growing from where the sun could not possibly shine.

Her colourful career as an art and music teacher concluded abruptly when, under her tutelage, one of her students persuaded a thirty-foot-long inflatable penis to wobble ominously through the window behind the headmaster's head as he was addressing a governors' meeting. She had then married one Timothy Smallpiece, the curator of a tiny art gallery in Sleephaven where her work was featured. One of her sculptures – a wicker basket containing a severed head on a bed of exotic fruits – memorably caused one elderly voyeur to pass out.

As she was ever a woman of lustful pleasures, her husband had passed away from exhaustion a few years before. Now she sat on her Celtic dragon throne chair, propped up by vermillion and gold cushions, and spent each day nagging the staff, scribbling incomprehensible poetry, and sailing on a sumptuous ocean of memories and pure invention. It was a constant voyage that she loved.

"Mason. Stop staring at that poor woman."

"Yes, mum. Gawd, I wouldn't want to end up like that," he remarked.

Miss B heard the remark. She pulled a wooden lever and her chair rotated to allow her a glimpse of Mason.

She composed a sinister and toothless smile that chilled Mason down to his boots. The smile evolved into a smirk, and finally a grin of such fiendishness that it, more eloquently than any words, expressed her feelings. *Thank God I never ended up like you*, she mused; and that was revenge enough for his insult. Miss B deeply savoured victories of the mind. As Mason's Adam's apple descended into his neck, Miss B lowered the lever and turned her attention once more to the joyous landscape.

She had been watching the storm's lightning fork the land. Its shifting ghostly drift across the valley and punishing needles of rain excited her spirits. Now the emergence of the sun's balm and kiss on the dripping trees and patient stones of the old house summoned joy from within her. The sun caught the blond hair of her favourite piano student as Yvonne entered the room. The light faded briefly as Yvonne bent down to kiss her.

"Mrs. Smallpiece. How are you?"

The old lady scribbled, "Call me Miss Bonkers. Or Miss B. How are you? Tell me about Alison."

And Yvonne did. She received a rapturous hug. But Miss B started scribbling again. It is about the young couple she saw from the window, sitting on the stile by the wooden gate, playing chess. An image of them appeared on the screen. Yvonne rushed to the window and looked back at Miss B, shaking her head. "Not there now," she said.

Miss B wrote, "They were there. And dogs."

Yvonne looked towards the woods, wistfully. "A young couple?"

We will leave them there in the fading afternoon light, talking among the eclectic scenery of Miss B's room: the William Morris prints; cushions of tulip, rose, and pimpernel; a carved oak armoire and dresser; deep ruby curtains; the stained-glass table supported by a carved dragon; the chess set of nemesis fairies and ghost mirror.

As Mason and his mother crept furtively from the room, they failed to notice that, on the plasma screen above Miss B's chair, the image of a gigantic three-toed sloth had appeared, crawling across a dystopian landscape. Curiously, it was wearing a Tranmere Rovers hoodie.

ANGEL OF THE NORTH

A rock star returns to her old school

Angel North glanced at the vast winged sculpture as the Newcastle Express streaked across the level plains and turfy fields of the Northumberland countryside. The monument's tilted arms stretched taut in divine entreaty, its steel face eyeless and feet rooted deep in ancient mineworkings. Angel saw the land rising as a wave to northern crags and fells beyond the glittering River Tyne – a jagged steel pin driven into England's flank, spiralling up to Kielder Burn and the rugged Cheviot Hills under the rising autumn sun.

As she watched, Angel felt herself slowly disengage from London's smothering embrace and choking fingers. A car would be waiting for her at Newcastle's grey Victorian station. "Something special for you, babe," her agent had said. "You'll love it. And your guitar and amp will be set up for you. Enjoy it!"

Angel's mother, Rose, had given her the name while lying alone and destitute in the Gateshead Maternity unit. It was her only meaningful gesture to a world that was harsh and grim and unloving and offered no hope. What would she think now as her daughter arrived at Wallsend Academy in a 1930 Daimler Drophead Coupe, creating something of a stir as it majestically swung into the staff car park?

Angel stepped from the Daimler's interior, blinking in the bright sun. All eyes were drawn to the purple hair, charcoal Lucy Yak dungarees, black boots and purple hoodie. Miss Starling, the principal, adorned in autumnal tones that melded perfectly with her office furniture, shook hands with this slender, chic woman. She possessed, Miss Starling noticed, the most startling green eyes beneath the flying violet and plum tresses but was, she felt, strangely uncertain. Angel's eyes flickered nervously across the ranks of assembled staff and students, whose blazers and coats were whipped by the unrelenting northern winds that scurried across the tarmac, hoisting crisp packets and drying autumn leaves into a frantic tumult.

It was the relentlessness of the sea gales and the splendour of the northern sky's auroras that had been the theatrical counterpoint to Angel's young life on the Wallsend housing estate and provided the frenzied emotions and unquiet music that had inspired her to write. She had played the guitar and piano relentlessly to herself, her only audience – after the death of her mother – to the quivering anger and urgency that had stalked her each day. Music was her only antidote to this perpetual haunting, at once menacing and energising. Now, as she stood, feeling the lash of the whipping winds, she wondered if she had been right to come. But she had something to return. It had to be done.

The grey doors of the Wallsend Music Suite unfolded as petals, exposing the inner sanctum of stage and performance space. The school's house banners fluttered up towards a steel atrium that allowed light to pour into the little auditorium of cushioned chairs and steel-grey carpet. Her heart fluttering, Angel walked towards the platform. As promised, the Fender Hellcat sat upright on its Mojo frame, the Yamaha amp with its twin speakers mounted on stands – impassive, silent witnesses; the Neuman microphone, angled like a dockyard crane, awaited. Amid a shuffling of feet, an audience of young and old assembled and slipped into their seats. Angel strode into the magic crucible of performance. She looked down at the faces, unknowing and wide eyed. "Good afternoon. You might know this song. It's called *Sister Mary*. It's about something that happened to a friend of mine."

Angel sang perfectly, holding the pathos of the song in her hand, her guitar playing crystalline and shimmering.

Sister Mary strays the riverbank; she walks alone,
casting into waters her virgin stone.
Will the sunlight break her secret
as she quietly kneels?
Sister Mary, tell me in the morning how you feel.

Does she still love? Does she still desire?
Does her heart inside burn just like a raging fire?
Does her life breathe on like
the silent depths of a wishing well?
Sister Mary, tell me in the morning how you feel.

Does she feel me now, far away and yet so near?
I'll be here every day, and I hope you will hear
the last few words I have to say to you:

Sister Mary, if the singing ever tires your voice,
if the incense fails to fix your mind to rejoice,
if when bells are tolling,
your heart no longer leaps to their peal.
Sister Mary, tell me in the morning how you feel.

Before her performance, Angel had gazed upon an audience of agog teachers and children, all of whom appeared to be badly in need of a holiday. The spluttering children and staff coughed and sniffed as tactfully as they could, but by the end they were mesmerised. They burst into a torrent of applause, the children rising to their feet, hands above their heads, eyes shining in admiration. This was one of their own, a Wallsend girl, making good. She had escaped and returned in triumph to consecrate this cultural chapel and claim it as her own.

"I cannot tell you how amazing it is to be standing here," Angel said. "I didn't know whether I should come back. I have so many memories. Not all are good. And there's a special reason I must keep as a secret for now. I can only speak the wise words my music teacher, Miss Hackett, spoke to me just before she retired. In fact, they were always written above her desk. 'Music gives a soul to the universe, wings to the mind, flight to the imagination, and life to everything.' I think that's true. She also said to me, 'The only truth is music,' and I believe that too."

The children beamed, and the staff held their breath. "Listen to your teachers, children. Miss Hackett was old, grumpy, and brilliant. And I owe her everything. Your teachers aren't celebrities. They don't dress in high fashion. They're women and men who love you and want you to change the world. They're the crucibles of genius." Another wave of applause engulfed the room. Angel stepped forward from behind the microphone and stood on the edge of the stage. The young faces hushed, gazing upward in awe.

"As a working-class girl from Wallsend, here among my community, my roots, my people, it gives me great pleasure to declare the Angel North Music Suite open!"

An ovation of clapping and cheering broke out as a wave across the auditorium. One child burst from the throng and ran to the stage before embracing Angel and presenting her with flowers.

* * *

"Put that down, Brenton. You know it just annoys the teachers."

Brenton pursed his lips, his eyes focusing on the Rubik's cube that spun in his hands, his fingers frenziedly twisting and working.

"Nah. I'm on! Got it! Got it! Yes!" Brenton Bramwell grinned. "Friedrich method, sir."

"Don't call me sir. I'm only a TA!" said Wahaj. "Can we do maths now, Brenton?"

The freckled grin returned to Brenton's face. "Just have been. You know it's like that thing, sir."

"I said don't … What thing?"

"That thing with wings, sir. When you took us. You said it was about the miners and the industrial revolution and our hopes, and stuff."

"Yes," said Wahaj.

"But it ain't, sir. It's like the cube. Solving it, sir. You don't have to have a puzzle. Do you, sir?"

"You mean the Angel of the North. I guess not, but why?"

"That artist, Gormley bloke. That were all rubbish. Just wanted to make an angel with big wings. He wanted to fly. Canny netty, that, like! But weren't no algorithm."

Wahaj studied Brenton's chubby face, the smear of dirt on his cheek. The toothy grin. The bulky black blazer that was too big for him, the bright button eyes, the stubby little nose. "Eh up, sir! What tha' reckon?"

"I reckon you need to stop playing with that thing at the start of every lesson. It just means you get sent to sanctuary and learn nothing."

"Nay, sir. Don't like lessons. They're cakky. Learn lots wi' thee sir. Know loads o' stuff."

Wahaj smiled. "You do."

"An' that woman. That singer. Angel North. Is she really here?"

"Yes."

"They reckon she used to go to Wallsend. Right canny lass. Your sort, sir. You were at this school then. Bet you kissed 'er."

"She's opening the new music suite."

"Room. Why call it a suite sir? Makin' another puzzle."

"Okay. It's a big room. With grey carpet, a stage, and posh chairs. With lots of little studios in it."

"Can I play my dad's trumpet in there, sir?"

"Of course."

Brenton grinned. "Bell's gone, sir. Clamming for me bait."

"Go get some food, Brenton. Maths after break. No more cube. Okay?"

Wahaj watched Brenton barge through the classroom door and join the corridor throng. A William Blake poster depicting Oberon and Titania became detached and floated to the floor. Wahaj reworked the Blu-tac and pressed the poster back on to the glass panel, leaving only a small gap around the edge for children's faces to peek into the room.

Wahaj sighed. Angel North. Angel Blenkinsopp that was. They had held hands in the bus shelter. They had shared a Mars bar and kissed stickily behind the caretaker's hut as the rain fell in grey columns. But they didn't care. Wahaj had watched Angel play netball, blond hair flying, and she had smiled at the attention. But then she had appeared in Hamlet. All the boys fancied her. Angel played Ophelia. Did the mad scene. Finger-picked guitar. Sports captain. Head girl. The teachers all spoke of her admiringly. That girl! Going places!

She stopped seeing Wahaj. In the school corridors, her eyes swept past him in search of more stimulating horizons. He saw her meeting a boy in the park; he wore an expensive dark leather jacket. Wahaj heard she was playing at The Metro Club, but he couldn't get a ticket. He stood outside in the drizzle, straining to look above the throng by the stage door. Couldn't get near her, past the wall of arty hangers-on.

Wahaj flicked open the maths workbook but memories had slipped impishly between its leaves and sent images flying across his vision. He felt Angel's fingers magically slide through his hair, her hand caress his cheek. "Is that a beard? Don't like it. I love your face. It's the colour of olives." And Wahaj was miraculously looking at her shimmering image in the workbook, her cheek as porcelain white as the page. "I wish …" he said aloud and glanced uncertainly at the door. Brenton would be back soon. He looked back at the page and she was gone.

* * *

Angel stood in Miss Starling's office, where she had so often been admonished for her makeup, ragged uniform, and her attitude towards Mr. Burke, the creepy business studies teacher who always wanted to "discuss her work" and asked, if she "was all right". She had memorably told him to "Eff off!" Now it was all different. The furniture was unchanged, but the aura of money and success induced a canine heat of sexuality and envy in the assembled company of bald male business owners and stressed middle-class wives, circling like old mongrels to imbibe the scent of stardom and luxuriate in the pungent aroma of cash.

Angel searched among their ranks for a sign of honesty and comprehension of what she had created, someone who could grasp and discuss her work and how it related to her life and her world. But pallid coffee, coronation chicken sandwiches and Garibaldi biscuits couldn't elevate this encounter to one of understanding and enrichment. Even so, she knew, in this desert of G Plan, plastic yuccas and galloping influenza, there lay a trembling heart and soul. In the arid conversation, she strained to listen for a distant, vibrating, urgent voice. Was he still here?

Miss Starling, Adele spectacles perched on her aquiline nose, fluttered across the study, and refilled Angel's cup from an aluminium teapot. "It must be so wonderful to travel. You must go to so many exciting places.

Angel responded bleakly. "A hotel is a hotel. An airport an airport. But an audience that wants to hear you is like nothing else. It's like a teacher who's really listening."

"If you want an audience, come perform at my club." Councillor Tippell, the chair of governors, ran a purple tongue along his shaggy cowboy moustache. He was the proprietor of the Stagecoach Rodeo Bar, *handily positioned in Gateshead Market! Howdy!* Tippell had famously initiated a stampede for the bar at the PTA's summer ball with his rendition of *Love Me Tender*, dressed in cowboy boots, full fringe jacket, rhinestone waistcoat, and a groaning leather belt with a silver buckle that struggled to contain his girth.

Angel beamed. "Not my genre, I'm afraid. But thank you."

"More shortbread?" Miss Starling proffered a tartan biscuit tin.

"No, thank you," said Angel. She breathed deeply and looked down.

"Is there anything else I can do?"

"Well, there is one thing you could do for me, Miss Starling."

Miss Starling smiled obsequiously. "Of course."

"I want to thank one of your colleagues. I owe him a great debt of gratitude."

"One of our staff? Who's that?"

"Mr Wahaj."

"Wahaj? Oh, yes. One of our teaching assistants. He's studying to be a teacher. He was a student here."

"Indeed. I have some of his property that I need to return personally. If I could spend a few moments with him, that would be perfect."

* * *

Brenton grasped the biro between his stubby fingers and bent over his exercise book. He removed his round spectacles and rubbed them with his handkerchief. "Eh up, sir. I'm fed up of this maths. Makin' my eyes go funny."

Wahaj was sitting on the corner of Brenton's desk and smiled down affectionately at the boy's tousled head. "You've done loads, Brenton. How are you managing with those glasses?"

"I dinna like these specs, sir. They mist up. Me mates call me Foggy Goggles!"

"Well, they look great on you. And you're learning."

Brenton wasn't listening. He was looking past Wahaj at the figure standing in the doorway. "Bloody 'ell. It's 'er!"

Wahaj turned. All the pain and grief and sorrow he had felt – and had spent years in trying to subdue – returned in an instant. But he was also deeply moved at the woman's hesitancy, her sense of standing on a precipice, of uncertainty, of some profound need. She spoke. "Miss Starling said I might find you here."

Transfixed, Wahaj stood up.

"Mr Wadger is always here, Miss," said Brenton. "Are you that woman? That Angel North bird?"

Angel stepped forward. "Yes, I am. I was hoping … What did you say your teacher's name was?"

"Oh, Mr Wadger. That were cos he dyed his hair for the school panto. It all went wrong. He were meant to be a tiger. Looked like a badger. So, we called 'im Wadger."

Wahaj looked down. Angel smiled and reverted to her Wallsend accent. "Aye, but I bet he's a right fine teacher, eh?"

"Aye, that's weird that. So posh on telly but tha' speaks like us."

"Brenton, you've worked so hard, I think you can go home a little early today. How's that?"

"Great, sir. Cheers. S'pose, you want to be alone, eh?" Brenton winked and looked at Angel. "Canny lass! Go on, sir. Give 'er a cuddle!"

"You've had a great day, Brenton. Don't spoil it. Now on yer bike!"

Brenton grinned and grabbed his bag and parka. "See you, Wadger!" he said, scuttling through the door.

"Seems a great kid."

"The worrying thing about Brenton is he seems to be able to read my mind!" Wahaj looked at Angel. She averted her eyes and was trembling. "I love that song, by the way. 'Sister Mary.'"

Angel smiled ruefully. "It's just a song about another girl who makes the wrong decision."

"Yes, when I heard it, I thought of ... of ... well ..." Wahaj was suddenly struggling with a desire to hold Angel.

"Look. Perhaps I shouldn't be here. But I just had to. Just had to!" Angel bit her lip and shivered. "Are you ... are you married?" Wahaj shook his head. "With someone?"

"No. There have been ... but no. No one."

"No one!" Angel moved closer, her hands reaching for him. "No one? But I need you to have someone. I need to know there's someone else." She grasped his shirt and gazed anxiously into his face.

"No one. I never wanted to."

"There must have been someone. There was, wasn't there?"

"No. No one who mattered. Or me to them. No."

"So, what do you do now?"

"I live alone."

"Alone."

"Yes. And I dream."

"Of what? Who?" They heard the sound of running feet in the corridor. Wahaj turned and caught the sight of Brenton's grinning face in the door window and heard laughter.

"Look, I'm going to have to lock the door. If we're going to talk like this. Okay?"

"Okay."

Wahaj turned the key in the lock. "We're alright for a bit, but I can't keep this door closed for long."

Angel drew him close again. "So ... you have no one. No one." A gasp of pain escaped her lips, and her arms grasped his waist. "Why, why, why? I need to know why."

"Look. We can't just stand here. I'm at work. Someone might come." He looked anxiously at the door. "The walls are like paper. Let's keep our voices down." He held her waist delicately and guided her into the corner by the book cupboard. Angel gasped gently at his touch and looked into his eyes.

"I still need to know why."

"Because I … I just couldn't. Without you. I was a fake. I faked it and tried to believe, but I was lying. And I knew. I wasn't going to mislead anyone. Pretend to love. Just couldn't."

Her green eyes startled, her gaze penetrating, all seeing. "Did you think I'd come back?"

"No, yes, no. No. I had faith. But I never expected this. I watched, listened, loved from afar. From my room. My tablet. My phone. And I prayed."

"Prayed?"

"Yes. I go to church. It helps me. I like someone talking to me about life once a week on a Sunday. It doesn't mean I believe anything. It just moves me forward. Until now."

"Hold me," Angel whispered. Wahaj hesitated. "Hold me. I insist. I'm breaking. I'm broken." Her arms wrapped around his shoulders. "I'm so tired. So, so tired of … not being me. You made me happy. Then I wanted more. Not to be me. And it's made me miserable. I'm so miserable. And I knew I needed to see you." Angel flung herself forward, her arms grasping Wahaj's shoulders, the purple storm of her hair flinging across his face.

"So good to hold you again." Wahaj kissed her cheek. "I wasn't expecting this. I thought you would visit and be gone. Just some PR stunt. And I would just stand. Watching. Like before."

Angel stroked his face. "Still got that beard. I like it better now. But I have to give you this." She reached into her hoodie pocket and produced a tiny case. "It's your ring. You gave it me." She gazed into his eyes, searching his features. Tears tumbled down her face. "I was fifteen. You pledged your love."

"I did."

"But you feel differently now?"

"You know how I feel. You know! I hope you haven't come back to taunt me. I couldn't bear it. Believe me."

"I'm returning this ring to you," Angel said decisively, and placed the case in his hand. "There!" They stood apart.

"Oh, right."

"It's yours."

"I gave it to you."

"No. It's yours." She pressed it into his hand and closed his fingers around the case.

"Okay."

"But ..." She wheeled away from him and stood on the other side of his desk. "But if you should want to give it me again. I just might say yes." She crossed to a display and contemplated a child's drawing of an elderly couple holding hands.

"Might. Maybe? Must I live on the edge?"

"Yes, yes, you must. Until you ask me."

"It was only a cheap ring."

"I know."

"I bought it at the market."

"More valuable than the gems of Ind. So, are you going to ask me?"

"I don't know. I'm not ready. Can't we talk?"

"We're talking. We *are* talking."

"Don't I get the chance to woo you again?"

"Woo? Jeez! Come on. Or I shall be gone into the great forever, the barren moon of the universe. The Sea of Tranquillity. Or the sea of clouds. Or the Oceanus Procellarum."

"Which is ...?"

"The Ocean of Storms. And I will die there. I will be gone. Among the stars I will perish. For now, I've returned. Fallen back to planet Earth. What is it to be, Wahaj?" Angel smiled ruefully. "Mr. Wadger? Did it mean nothing?" She stood defiantly, hands on hips, daring him to act. "We Geminis are smart, sharp, and needy. I can't wait. Be my twin!" Wahaj opened the case. The thin gold ring glowed, the twin pillars of the Dioscuri gleaming from the bezel.

Someone tried the door handle. Brenton's impish eyes peeped under the poster.

"We can't stay here. We need to go. He moved towards the door, but Angel's arm caught his wrist. "Remember. Remember your pledge to me."

"I do remember." Breathing deeply, he moved towards her.

"It was raining." Angel smiled. "In the bus shelter."

"Should we go back there?"

"No, here. There's no need. I just need to know now. I can't go back on that train without having been changed. Transformed. By you." Wahaj and Angel gazed at each other. Her hands were on his waist. Her lips were light on his. Then stronger. He felt the energy, the power of their affection, and they were back in the bus shelter on Dog Lane, sitting on the swings in Wallsend Park in the twilight, under the silver moon, on the top deck of the 98 bus to Gateshead. At the base of the steps in the school library.

"Now, please," murmured Angel. "Now. Just whisper it to me."

* * *

Angel North's descent into Wallsend had caused something of a stir in the stolid Geordie press and media, which was addicted to a daily diet of chav racers, pub punch-ups, or the latest bobby-dazzler to sign up for The Magpies. Startled from their reverie, the Tyneside press pack poured into black cabs and streamed for unfashionable Wallsend, with its avuncular post-war council estates, cramped Victorian workhouses, and Edwardian terraces. Journalists and TV crews gathered on the pavement of Victory Road; their lenses aimed like a firing squad towards the academy's steel driveway gates.

Portly mums with strollers chatted and vaped while students clustered in blazered groups outside Gupte's

Newsagents, Wishywashy's Launderette, and the Codfather Fish Bar. Beyond the gates, the gleaming Daimler waited in the staff car park, in sharp contrast to the motley auto jumble of third-hand Fords, Nissans, battered VW camper vans, and mopeds.

Angel and Wahaj emerged from the classroom and stepped into the bright corridor. Wahaj hesitated. "Shouldn't we go back to Miss Starling's office? To say goodbye?"

Angel shook her head. "No, I've said that. We should go. Now." She grasped Wahaj's hand and urged him towards the door.

Brenton marched cheerfully out of the boys' toilets, where he'd been standing on a cistern with his ear to the wall. "Sorry, sir. You've got to marry her now. I've texted me mates."

"You what?" Wahaj was open-mouthed. Beyond the playground they saw the gathering crowd in Victory Road. Angel held up her ring finger; Brenton wasn't impressed. "Eh up, sir. Tha's a tight git. My mother sells them down t'market."

"You were listening to a private conversation," said Wahaj, pushing open the fire door.

"Don't worry, sir," said Brenton. "I couldn't hear that much. I'd keep clear o' that Ocean of Storms, though."

"We're going!" said Wahaj. He and Angel began a fast-weaving walk through the multicoloured miscellany of staff vehicles. The door of the Daimler swung open. A smiling chauffeur in a smart grey uniform sprang to attention and opened the rear door.

Angel stopped. "No, Wahaj." The wind blew her hair across her face, and she smiled up at him. "I want you to take me in your car. Leave the Daimler here."

"I wouldn't do that, miss," said Brenton. "Won't have no wheels left by mornin'!"

"My car? Are you sure?"

"Nay, miss. Sir's only got a hippie wagon. Nice, though. Got a big flower on it and some furry dice."

Wahaj clasped Angel's hand and led her to his aged VW camper. "Perfect," said Angel, surveying the hand-painted orange-and-yellow bodywork, as well as the travel stickers clustered in the side windows. When the door creaked open, Angel stepped up into the boho interior and settled in the canvas seat, draped with beads and a cerise throw. She closed the door and wound down the window. Brenton's cheeky face grinned up at her.

"I don't mind if you heard what we said, Brenton." She beamed down at the chubby boy. "Anyway, I'll be back. I'll teach you to sing."

"Aye. Thank you, miss. Fancy you'll only try the once."

Wahaj appeared in the driver's seat and turned the ignition. "Have a good half term, Brenton. And keep out of trouble. Give your mum my best wishes."

"Yes, sir. Kinna come to weddin'?"

"See you, Brenton."

The van slid forward and swung towards the exit. Brenton hitched up his tie and strode stoutly in front. "Eh up! Open sesame," he shouted to the bewildered caretaker, who promptly set about opening the gates. "Thanks, Mr Milburn." Brenton marched into the middle of Victory Road and held up his hand to the assembled photographers. "Now just wait," he shouted. "You'll get yer chance." A bus screeched to halt, and Brenton waved the VW into the road. A salvo of clicking cameras and swinging lenses ensued. The tubby mums and raggedy dads picked up their phones to capture the moment and hoisted infants on to their shoulders.

"Aw, look at 'em. Bless."

"Is that Mr Wadger?"

"Go on, sir. Big smackerooney on the gob."

"Eee, in't that lovely?"

"Wonder if they'll 'ave the widding in Wallsend."

"Nay, lass. Don't be daft."

"Eh, Mr Wadger is going to marry that Angel?"

"Lucky bugger."

"I'd marry 'im any day. I'm fed up of you!"

As they drove towards the station, Radio Bliss FM's afternoon DJ, Elvis – *Feel the Heat!* – Purvis, was playing back-to-back hits by "our local lass and rock legend, Angel North". "Word has it, she's come to Wallsend to rekindle an old flame," he announced. As Wahaj's battered camper van trundled into Newcastle station, a Mr Brenton Bramwell – "who knows the couple *intimately*" – was about to be interviewed *live* from Wallsend Academy.

THE SWARM

Watching a group of grown men trying to punch each other is – viewed from a safe distance – an entertaining spectacle. Not least because the combatants are usually unbelievably bad at the actual techniques of pugilism. I can recall, as a student, waking from a lunchtime snooze against a tractor wheel to find the other farm workers engaged in a monumental fistfight. The biggest one had called the littlest one a short arse. Much grunting, swearing, and flailing until a blow did land, exploding the prodigious proboscis of the largest, florid-faced man.

Being a football fan sometimes leads you into alien territory. A visit to Millwall in the 1970s left me with the spectacle of over a hundred football fans teeming over the recumbent bodies of Crystal Palace supporters. There was no holding them. They were part of a swarm. They had surrendered their individuality to be part of a bigger movement, a primeval collective who knew nothing other than to swing punches to claim their territory. Defend their nest. It emerged later that the reason was the desire of the Palace fans to have a beer in what Millwall fans regarded as one of *their* pubs.

Watching a group of men, you have employed to build a wall in your garden, trying to slap each other while appearing to be dancing on hot coals, is different. It takes surrealism to a new level. But there they were, Willy, Dim Nigel, 'The Boy' and Rufus-the-Beard, clad in work boots, overalls, and woolly hats, floating like butterflies and smacking like St Trinian's schoolgirls.

I'd been meaning to get rid of the wasps' nest in the earth bank at the rear of the garden. I had been buzzed a few times while strimming the brush and decided to resort to napalm. I ordered Terminator Wasp Eradicator foam. It was like a machine pistol, with a canister magazine, an evil-looking red handle and trigger attachment. That was as far as I got. Men like me have never grasped that buying the weapon is not the same as solving the problem by actually pulling the trigger. Token gestures. Love them.

I had made the mistake of going on Facebook and received a torrent of heart-rending pleas for a stay of execution from people with gardens so vast their wasps could easily be ignored – or, more likely, quietly exterminated by their grumpy gardeners. And so, the innocent little angels were taken off death row. These were *virtuous* earth-burrowing wasps, *Vespula vulgaris* – ground-diggers – that, one deluded soul assured me, do not sting; and they were the *gardener's best friend*, feeding on all manner of garden pests.

They were so *green* and *cultured*, apparently, I began to think that the little sods must also be fluent in Latin and liked opera – Madame blooming Butterfly, no doubt! And so, I sat in the garden with Biggles, our dachshund; we watched the wasps come streaming in squadrons from their dark earth den, like Battle of Britain heroes, sporting goggles and stripy jumpers, to do battle with the invading hordes of Hun-Aphids crossing the channel. There were pitched battles every day above the dancing marigolds, long-tongued zucchini flowers and the nodding fronds of Charlotte and Desirée potatoes.

There was one particularly fierce conflict where, frankly, the Jerries took one hell of a beating, above the nasturtiums – heroically guarding the broccoli from daylight raids by fascist greenfly and marauding cabbage-white butterflies. I watched all this while lying on a sunbed with our dachshund Biggles, drinking beer, as the insects whirled in dizzying circles. At dusk, I noticed, the warriors streamed back to base to discuss the day's kills and mourn the loss of comrades. "Yes, Buzzer bought it I'm afraid. Over the leeks. Damn shame!"

My wall-building artisans looked at me balefully when I took them cups of tea. "You didn't tell us about they buggers," said Dim Nigel, his woolly hat nodding towards the bank.

"Sorry lads," I said, and scurried off for some ointment. Willy had copped one in a particularly nasty place. The neighbours had watched him frantically removing his trousers before running out of the garden and leaping into his battered van.

Autumn turned to winter and spring was trying on her new bonnet. This February morning, I walked across the ragged lawn and approached the bank, carrying a glittering new shovel. The time had come.

I plunged the blade into the bank, above the dark entrance. The grass clump gave way and tumbled on to the lawn. I expected to find a giant papery nest with grubs, but the entrance to a cavern had appeared. The interior of the bank had been sculpted out around a dry-stone wall, creating a huge cavity. I hesitated, before climbing on to the roof of the hollow.

I lowered my spade and levered up the sod. Inserting my fingers under the edge of the loosened turf, I ripped it from the surrounding network of fibrous roots, before hurling it to the base of the bank. I stared down into the cavity.

An alien city, a paper mâché globe, a Death Star, was clinging to the sheltered side of the old stone wall. A thing of sinister military precision, it clung like an unexploded bomb to the stones. I gulped and crudely stuck the spade-tip into the grey orb. A chunk of the casement fell away, revealing a layered metropolis, a breeding colony of menacing wafers and husks, each cell dark with an insect embryo.

I marvelled at the precision engineering of this grey crucible. It was also horrifying. A cramped world of layered lives, that would soon emerge as a swarm – a single destructive entity. Creatures that could not reason, whose absolute loyalty to the cause of self-preservation, of protecting the home, was wired into their DNA. As part of a pre-eminent species, was I going to kowtow, allow these stripy brigands to sink their venom into my grandchildren? Was I going to permit *the swarm*? I thought of the tin with the red trigger.

Time to go nuclear.

I strode into the greenhouse. The yellow canister gleamed from the bench. Time to man up! I snatched the can as a rain squall arose from the sea, a grey phantom, and swarmed over the garden. In my glasshouse, a sudden drumbeat of raindrops, and the panes transformed to shimmering water streams and mirages. I sniffed the air. It was divinely scented with garlic and basil.

Reluctantly, I fumbled for my spectacles and read the instructions on the tin.

"Use at night when wasps are less active." Seemed like a good idea. All those little wasplets tucked up in their sticky sleeping bags, while mummy wasp – a prodigiously striped creature, the size of a giant yellow courgette – gazes menacingly upon her vast brood, her mandibles slavering and antennae twitching.

At night, eh? I could sneak out under cover of blanket dark, a woolly-hatted silent assassin, covered head to foot, carrying what appeared to be a deadly machine pistol. But there were drawbacks. Supposing the moon suddenly swamped the garden with white light; our neighbours would not see a bold assassin, but a startled animal frozen in the act of apparently committing a terrible atrocity.

But there were other little local difficulties. The memsahib and I always partake of a few snifters as the sun stretches down for the horizon. So, my twilight scamper with a lethal weapon could have some unfortunate consequences; climbing the slippery stone steps, scaling the bank, or tripping over the hosepipe, could all leave me lying on my back – limbs flailing, like a hapless dung beetle. Finding the wasps' nest in the dark could also be tricky. A torch beam might arouse them into full vindictive buzziness. Suppose I found the wrong hole and gave a particularly grumpy badger a sharp squirt of pyrethrin while he was having a snooze. Or a family of adders fancied a late snack?

Hmm. I removed my spectacles and placed the gun under the bench.

Leave it to nature….

PANDORA'S DOOR

The oak-panelled pantry door had been Duluxed gleaming white. Behind the door lay an Aladdin's cave of sweet treats, jars of mincemeat, slices of almond shortcake, succulent dried fruit in jars, chocolate bonbons and sherbet fountains. Blonde macaroons and cupcakes dimpled with cherries and peel. Or leftover pork crackling, pudding bowls of beef dripping that concealed their secret wells of succulent meat jelly – salty and tongue-dripping; the single leftover glistening lamb cutlet, mint-clinging, fat gleaming as white as the painted door. "Eat me! Eat me!" it begged.

My sister had been waiting for her chance. Mum had told Pandora off about her secret larder incursions. I had decided it was time to make a stand. Cunning as a blonde fox, she virtuously finished the washing up, a halo hovering about her pixy-bobbed head, as Mum sighed, snatched the car keys from the hook and dashed out the back door to collect Dad from the station. I trembled and shuffled between the television and the sliding door, just ajar, ready to witness her brazen looting of the larder's hidden gems. I had been reading about Carthage being sacked and looted by the Romans in my *Boys Today Encyclopaedia*. Tonight, unlike the hapless Carthaginians, I would be ready.

I sat in front of the TV watching *This Is Your Life* with the sound muted. The latch on the heavy larder door clicked. I bolted from my seat and sprang through the sliding door. Extending my left arm, I slammed the larder door shut. An astonished blonde stared down at me.

"What you doin'?"

"This has to stop."

"Who says?"

"I do. Mum told you not to."

"She doesn't mind. Now get out the bleedin' way."

143

"No." I spreadeagled myself across the door. "Mum told you not to."

"Oh, piss off. I'll share it with you."

"No."

"You can have half a macaroon."

"No. I don't want it."

"A whole *effing* macaroon."

"No."

"No? You don't want a whole macaroon! You're a boy! A pig in short trousers."

"I'm not moving!"

Pandora grabbed my wrist and tried to prise my fingers from the door handle. I stamped on her foot.

There was a yelp and shriek and she hopped backwards before lunging at me. We locked hands and struggled; Pandora twisted my arm up my back. I kicked her with my heel and an ugly wrestling match ensued which ended abruptly when the coal scuttle intervened. It crashed to the floor sending dust and grey coke nuggets tumbling across the pristine kitchen tiles.

"Now look what you've done," Pandora said. "I'll tell Mum!"

"Wasn't me. You kicked it."

"Oh, bollocks! I hate brothers! Open the effing larder."

"Why?"

"Cos the dustpan and brush is in there, shit-brain!"

I swung open the door and Pandora grabbed the dustpan and snatched a macaroon. "Greedy cow!"

"Ha! My reward for clearing up your crap!"

When Mum returned, she stared in bewilderment at the kitchen floor. "You washed it. Why?"

There was a tense silence. "My fault, Mum," I said. "I knocked over the coal scuttle. "Pandora shot me a glance. It was full of love.

"You been fighting again," said Mum. "I told you not to. And don't you look so innocent, madam! Why would little Johnny knock over the coal scuttle?"

"Oh, so it's my fault. Always is!" Pandora stormed out of the kitchen to her room. A bedroom door slammed.

Mum shook her head. "I just don't know what's going on in that girl's head."

I knew. Even then. Always in trouble. Doors. Doors being slammed. Close off this. Don't do that.

Later, I crept into Pandora's room.

"What do you want?" she murmured from beneath the eiderdown.

"I want to be with you. My skin and blister. I'm sorry." I knelt beside her bed. She was clutching her comfort blanket and had her thumb in her mouth. I kissed her forehead. There were tear tracks on her cheeks.

"I hate it here, she said. "When I'm sixteen, I'm going. Far away on a big ocean liner. With a man."

I panicked. "Don't leave, Pandora. Don't. Please," I whispered.

"Just read to me, then, little brother." She passed me a battered paperback. *From Russia with Love*. A page had been folded back. "A juicy bit. Give it some welly."

And so, I read the section where James Bond returns to his hotel to find the stunningly beautiful blonde Tatiana making sure his bed was nice and warm. My recitation was a study in schoolboy bewilderment; I could only assume that Tatiana – like any mean sister – had already guzzled his bedtime cocoa. It also seemed she had no pyjamas. All this while Pandora looked at the ceiling and dreamt.

Looking back, I don't think I learned very much from my schoolteacher, Mrs Panzetta. She was huge and wore a long grey dress down to her mighty ankles. She would stride about the classroom, the dress swinging like a church bell. Pandora was a *much* more interesting teacher. She taught me how to read, and how to draw. Pandora could do watercolour landscapes. She did a cartoon of our horrible grandmother with big square glasses and a dead fox slumped around her shoulders. It made me laugh.

I did have to explain to my mother what a copy of *Casino Royale* was doing on my bedside table. "Did Pandora give you that?"

"No," I lied. "I found it in the school library. Mrs Panzetta said I could read it." It was rapidly replaced by *The Secret of Skull Mountain*. Boring as hell. There were no girls in it. I heard mum telling Pandora off, again.

Then, Pandora told me about snogging. It happened a lot in the books she asked me to read. I didn't like the sound of it. But it was alright. Big Marjory at the primary school taught me to snog her behind the toilets because it was her birthday. I liked it after that.

Then some men came to the house. The pantry door was taken away and thrown on to a heap. Dad was going to burn it. The men replaced all the kitchen furniture with Formica cupboards that had doors of fake wood. Mum was really pleased. Dad was in the garage using his workbench. The pantry door was laid out under an arc light like a patient in an operating theatre, as he sandpapered and planed it into shape. "John. You do this!" He handed me a tin of linseed oil and a brush, and I slowly drew the paintbrush across the wood grain, savouring the unlocked fragrances of sandalwood and cinnamon. I loved the fresh flaxseed smell of the oil and marvelled as, with each brushstroke, the grain darkened from pale pine to burnished gold.

The door became my new desk. Dad had crafted the legs and drawers, and the desk was berthed like a ship of state beneath the bedroom window that looked on to the garden. The house would suddenly fill with uncles and aunts and cousins and grannies, and they would all troop through my bedroom to admire it. I had to sit at the desk pretending to write or draw or read some huge tedious encyclopaedia while they trailed their fingers across the surface or opened the drawers and asked me dim questions about "wasn't I proud of it" and "what was I going to do when I grew up"?

Pandora was jealous. But she had a white dressing table with three mirrors and a white pouf; and the top was always covered with weird-looking pots and tubs and bottles and hairbrushes and curling tongs and hairbands and tissues and a jewellery box and powders that made me sneeze. She didn't need a desk as well, Dad said. So, she used mine.

Mum and Dad were armchaired, slippered and grumpy TV watchers. Mum's hairnet covered an armoury of hair curlers, clustered like projectiles, while Dad chewed his false teeth or puffed his pipe, sending blue plumes of Old Holborn smoke drifting towards the ceiling. They would lecture newsreaders and politicians, competing to denounce anything that spoke of an evolving world that was shifting around their semi-detached dream like a forest on the march. Mick Jagger appearing in full lipstick singing *Let's Spend the Night Together* resulted in us both being sent to our rooms, while Bob Dylan's *The Times They Are a-Changin'* induced a paroxysm of shared rage. This was not the land they had fought for.

Pandora's boyfriends started coming to the house. They would stand in the hall as if waiting for the dentist. Mum would grunt as she walked past. Sometimes they would disappear into Pandora's room and play The Beatles or Elvis on the red and white Dansette. One looked like James Dean. And he had a car. He lasted longer than the others.

Then it happened. There was a battered suitcase in the hall. Pandora told us she was going. She had had enough. Too many effing rows and she was always in the wrong. Exhausted, Mum and Dad lowered their gaze and stared at their dinner plates. She was going to meet Paul and they were going away. She hugged me, and I smelled the *Oh! De London* perfume that Paul had given her for Christmas. I cried that night alone in my room, the desk gleaming in the moonlight.

There is more I need to tell you but cannot. The years have gone, and I could only watch Pandora's life from afar. I cannot really explain what has happened to her. I can record all the events, but the problem is not the facts. The problem lies in composing the truth. And I cannot achieve a command over the words that might tell you how this all feels. Pandora has Covid-19 and is in a hospital far away and I simply do not know what to do with this grief and fear. There is another door that I do not want her to open, and I cannot stand in front and spread myself like a hapless crucifix to prevent her from passing through the doorway into the dark.

I still have the desk. It is in front of me now as I write. The drawer sticks and the tenon joints are creaking. Its surface – now the colour of oak – bears the scratches and stains and scrapes of time. I have decided to take the desk into my workshop. I will remove the legs and joinery. I will liberate the sandalwood resins and perfumes, and sand and scrape the surface until it is white again. I will bleed my energy and mind into the wood grain's graceful architecture of curving lines and swirls. The print of my fingers and heart and body will be an eternal presence across its grain and will bear my kiss of faith.

There is a cabin in the garden where the grandchildren come to stay. We call it Caspian's cabin. The room, where they all play and tumble and dream and talk their childhood jazz and nonsense and wisdom, will have a new door.

Pandora's door.

OUR MAN IN KAMPALA

The Uganda Diaries

I want to tell you about the time Mike and I went to Uganda. The visit was primarily to build on the joint work by our college and Ndeeba Senior Secondary School students in art, geography and English. The British Council funded the trip. I want to write about these wonderful projects, and how they are benefiting our students, in some detail. But first, there is the enigma of Uganda itself. If you have been there, you will know.

If not, you will need to make the journey we made and see what we saw. In particular, the story of Grace Nantagya and his family needs to be heard. His story is the story of Uganda, a vibrant ebullient nation rising to its feet after years of monstrous oppression and unimaginable violence. Grace and his family are not heroes but survivors, bright lights burning out of the dark time of fear and death and evil.

As Englishmen, conscious of our colonial past, we arrived in Entebbe airport and gazed up at a fabulous starlit African sky. We had travelled armed to the teeth against malaria, yellow fever, polio, dysentery, mosquitoes, and whatever dark peril lay ahead. Our hosts gathered us into cars, and we fired off into the dark to Mukono (yes, we had read the Foreign Office advice not to travel on the Entebbe to Kampala road at night because of robbers). Grace was our driver. White taxis sped past, their hazard lights flashing to celebrate the return of a distant relative. For us the adventure had begun, and we would accept, like wide-eyed schoolboys, whatever this verdant, virile nation would reveal.

We went to Ndeeba, worked with the students, trod the rain forest, were awestruck at the Nile's source, goggled at the equator, bounced through a game park in a rickety minibus, fought five-inch scarlet cockroaches in the shower, dined with the Bishop, confronted the street children of Kampala, and rocked to Afrigo. All this cannot be told without Grace's story, because nothing makes sense without it.

Grace is thirty-two. He teaches geography at Ndeeba. His wife, Irene, works in the university bookshop in Kampala. Grace and Irene have been married for four years. They have six children, three are their own. Richard (football and Manchester United mad) aged ten, Cynthia, eight, and Vanessa, five. Cynthia wrote a letter to me full of sparkling excitement at our arrival. They have three children from Grace's brother's marriage. Robbers murdered his brother and his wife – Grace's brother recognised one of the thieves. They showed no mercy. The children automatically became Grace and Irene's. In Uganda, your brother's children *are* your children. But Grace is one of only three surviving children from a family of twelve. His brothers and sisters have died from various causes including aids. Aids is rampant in Uganda. Four million people out of twenty-three million have HIV. No family is untouched.

Grace and Irene live in a neat bungalow to the south of Kampala. They have a garden to grow sweet bananas, vast pineapples and watermelons. In Uganda, a garden is for food not flowers. A Friesian cow proudly grazes the front lawn. Friends and relations live and work nearby. A beautiful tiny church is along the track, with the half-built Sunday school. A tumble of hand-made bricks is on hand for the next phase of construction. From a small white bungalow, a young priest does God's work, bumping along the red dusty tracks on a pushbike. At the end of Grace's lane, there is a chaotic crossroads of small square shops; boys on motorcycles wait for passengers, men lounge in the doorway of the barber's shop, and Ugandan reggae thuds from two giant home-made speakers outside a rickety record store.

This is Grace's community – where the Christian faith is as natural as breathing in a country whose people have had every cause to pray during the last thirty years. Two weeks before our visit, Grace's family woke in the night to find their home being entered. An intruder was cutting through the iron grille that Grace had used fortify his dining room window. Grace and his family could only tolerate this latest of several intrusions. Twenty young men with masks entered his home, one carrying a gun he had 'hired' from a corrupt policeman. They took anything of value, Grace's new shoes, the CD player he had bought when visiting my school in the UK, and even the watch bought for little Vanessa. No point in fighting: just let it happen or they will kill you. Having met the Natangyas, the injustice of it all is shocking.

As a young boy, Grace and his family had to learn to hide. One night he hid in the plantation with his mother as Idi Amin's crazed army ransacked the neighbourhood, stealing, raping and burning. They hid in the plantation for three days having placed their black-and-white TV in an earth-burrow for safekeeping. When the inept Milton Obote was in power, the president told the people "if the army comes to your house, give them half of what you have". Mass looting, violence and murder was the result. Since 1986, President Museveni and the National Resistance Movement have restored peace and stability.

The children are fed and go to primary school. Even in the slum areas, the children look happy and well. There is still crime, and the police are cheerfully corrupt. They may stop your car and demand money on the pretext that you have been driving too fast. Grace even arrested the 'chief' burglar himself and took him to the police station. The man was locked up for three days then presumably paid the police for his release. That said, Grace acknowledges that police pay, and conditions of work are poor. But it's better than before. Grace hopes that Museveni will stay in power – if not, "would the British like to return?"

Ndeeba Senior Secondary School – with its cheery motto *No Pains, No Gains* – is situated in a beautiful rural area not far from the Nile, on the Kampala-Jinja Highway. Within the immediate area there are seven churches and two mosques. The students pay £60 a term from the meagre subsistence farm incomes of their dedicated parents. Their hunger for learning is intense and the greatest lesson we in the UK can learn.

Two-piece Suits and Christianity

The imprint of the British in Uganda has had some peculiar results. Two of our most successful exports have been two-piece suits and Christianity. Why Ugandans took to both with such enthusiasm baffles me. Before these unwanted aspects of colonialism arrived, they had clothes, a rumbustious monarchy, and faith.

In the countryside, the women wear marvellously elegant floral dresses with puffed shoulders and sashes of silk. These same women can move with consummate elegance and style in these vivid garments while carrying a jerry can of water on their heads, armfuls of fruit, and sedate babies on their backs. No shopping trolleys, Mothercare pushchairs, and helpful husbands for them. We stopped to photograph some women emerging from their gardens. The smiled shyly and protested that they weren't looking their best.

In Kampala, the suit rules and some designer shops have appeared. Mind you, going into a shop to buy a suit is not essential. Walk along the pavement, and men will rush up to you with a two-piece suit, holding it against you as you walk. Shirt, sir? Certainly, sir. In fact, if you were to stand in your underwear outside the Uganda National Bank, within twenty yards you could acquire a complete outfit, and someone to polish your shoes to complete the effect. The suit is it. Get a suit and you are like the Europeans. I wore a suit on the first day of my visit to Ndeeba and simmered like a pressure cooker in the 87F heat. Even the teachers wore suits. Lebison Semmambo – the Headmaster of Ndeeba Senior Secondary School – spotted my distress. "You don't need to wear a suit,

John," he said gently. Next day, this saintly man came in a safari shirt.

Mike and I avoided the souvenir T-shirts and headed to a clothes shop owned by one of Grace's relatives. Beautiful handmade shirts and dresses festooned the walls and blossomed in doorways. I bought a wonderful traditional shirt in sumptuous gold and purple that would be out of place in drab old England. It will come out for high days and holidays. Grace gave me his wedding gown as a present. A flowing white silk tunic that suited him much more than a pallid, portly Englishman – I accepted it with deep gratitude. Ugandan weddings are quite something. There is a separate send-off party for the bride and the groom, and two weeks later the wedding itself, which everybody in the entire district attends if they bring some food or drink or gift to the event.

The wedding contains a marvellous piece of drama. The bride's aunt has the daunting task of persuading the bride's father that she is ready for marriage. He feigns a grumpy reluctance.

Aunt: (Pleading) Irene is a grown woman now. She is ready to leave home.

Father: (Grumpy) Who says she is ready to leave home?

Aunt: (Ignoring his utterly fatuous question – as if it wasn't obvious! But still speaking in soothing tones) She has fallen in love. She wishes to marry.

Father: (Even more grumpy) Where is this man she wishes to marry?

(A logical question since there is an audience of approximately five hundred men sitting sporting identical white silk tunics.)

The bride answers the question by placing a garland of flowers around the neck of the chosen one – it must be a tense moment for the groom, especially if the bride has forgotten her spectacles. The great thing is that the marriage takes place when the couple can afford to marry – they have often had children by then. So, the Christian concept of chastity before marriage is neatly nudged aside by the realities of simply affording a wedding.

Another Christian idea that failed to fully take root was marriage to one wife. Ugandan men often have three or even more wives. Grace remembers how his father would sometimes be gone from home for a few weeks as he visited another of his wives. In those terrifying times with Idi Amin's army on the loose, it would have added to his fear. Grace says he will only ever be married to Irene. Perhaps that is why his children and the adopted children of his brother are so happy and full of life.

Certainly, the idea of being married to only one wife passed by the Kings of Buganda[1], one of whose number accumulated the splendid total of 84 wives and 109 concubines. When the King was away from his palace – doubtless in search of more wives – some of his spouses were prone to dallying with unwise courtiers. The unfortunate Romeos were promptly castrated and banished to the bottom of the hill, where they had the appalling task of digging out a lake for the King with their bare hands. Mike and I saw the King's Lake. It is enormous and must have been created by a veritable army of eunuchs. The errant wives fared rather better, being banished to a pleasant villa at the side of the lake where they could watch the labours of their now less complete lovers. No, the top job in Buganda had to be King or *Kabbaka* – provided you could stand the pace.

I'm still puzzling about the impact of religion in Uganda and how it seems, improbably, to have made an

---

[1] Buganda is one of the old kingdoms in Uganda. The old monarchy was revived by President Museveni as a way of holding the country together. The present king has some power over matters within the kingdom. Grace told us that when he met the King, Grace instinctively dropped to his knees and bowed. The King's white palace had been looted and vandalised by Obote's soldiers. Grace has contributed to the appeal to restore the palace.

absolute connection with Ugandan culture and values. It's as likely as tossing a coin that comes down heads five thousand times in a row. Kampala has its Roman Catholic cathedral, Mosque, and a red brick Anglican Cathedral cloned from the southeast of England. An English choir was trilling and warbling as we wandered by their parked 4*4s and Morris Oxfords. From the top of the hill, the Cathedral breathed its awesome love over the slum Katanga district while the voices of the singers evoked ethereal and spiritual wealth above more basic needs. The silhouette of the Catholic cathedral is as ominous, like a pocket battleship parked on a hill.

Above the new university there is a religious building that sends hope and prayer flooding through your heart. The Bahai temple has nine doors, one for each of the world's religions. It is for all people. Its pure architecture *is* a prayer in execution, symmetry, inclusiveness, peace. It reminded me of the mantra *Give, sympathise, control.* In a world desperate to know itself, here was the answer and prayer was as natural as breathing. Bahai's believe that heaven and hell are not places, but states of being. Heaven is nearness *to* God; hell is separation *from* God. Heaven is presence of spiritual qualities. Hell is the absence of these qualities, or imperfection. "So powerful is the light of unity that it can illuminate the whole earth," a small poster proclaimed. We seem to spend so much energy looking for answers when all we need to do is look at each other.

Ants! Ants!

The Colline Hotel rises proudly above the frenetic main street of Mukono town. From our rooms on the sixth floor – the visit was funded by the British Council – we could look out across the white roofs to the teeming road where rows of trucks gleamed like insects on the march. Black telephone lines and power cables strung the dusty road. Behind the hotel were neat, prolific gardens of great pineapples and jack fruit.

Little white bungalows set in terracotta plantations of sweet bananas and mangoes. Occasionally a truck lurched up a country lane sending a red dust squall into the bright air.

We had arrived in Uganda armed to the teeth with every form of pill, potion, sunblock, insect repellent, and fortified by multiple injections. I was constantly expecting to be infected, stung, or bitten by some hidden menace. The white mosquito net draped over my bed like a gigantic wedding veil, didn't inspire confidence as I gazed from my bed like a ghastly reincarnation of Miss Haversham. The squawks and twitters of the local wildlife tend to make one rise early. Sliding from beneath the mosquito net I headed for the bathroom to do battle with a shower that had a mind of its own.

All was well until something crawled over my foot. A malevolent red-backed six-inch long cockroach was scurrying across the bath. Emitting a shriek, I resorted to panic and sprayed the monster with shaving foam before applying the shower head to maximise the effect. Poor cockroach. Having ascended six floors of the hotel to say *hello* he was banished to whence he came in a foaming ball of Brut. It seemed appropriate. Technology had triumphed.

Mind you, mosquitoes and bugs are more of a threat in England or Spain than Uganda. In the countryside Acholi cattle sporting huge bow-shaped horns chew happily, and children trek to boreholes for water with bare feet, heedless of thorns and snakes. Uganda is a benign and wonderful place, where gardens are for growing magnificent fruit and vegetables – not flowers (something they regard as curious and bizarre). Houses are for the rising middle class and the rich. Most of the rural people live in simple square structures of brick or block where they sleep – the rest of the time they live outside. With a constant temperature of 87F, who wants to be inside? Well, maybe in the rainy season. Storms are spectacular events: layers of ominous purple darken the sun as a prelude to earth-shaking thunder, lightning, and spears of rain. The storm seems to wait before it unleashes, as if choosing a target.

No, you have to go looking for any real threats to one's health and wellbeing – apart, that is, from being daft enough to decide to swim at the source of the Nile or plunge in to the Kalagala falls. The surging power of the waters travelling down Kalagala and Bujagali falls is awesome to behold. As we posed for photos on a rock close to the torrent we were warned – one slip would mean certain death. There is a plan to build a hydro-electric dam here; the country needs the energy, but there were protests from across the world about the project. Grace explained how important it was for the economy of this beautiful but impoverished area – Uganda has fourteen other sites as beautiful and dramatic. Isn't it better than burning fossil fuels to create electricity?

The source of the Nile is disfigured by a grotesque attempt by Idi Amin to build a house on stilts above the majestic waters. Clearly the great river had other ideas, and the concrete foundations are just visible below the surface as testimony to Amin's hideous folly.

A trip to the Mabira tropical rain forest between Mukono and Jinja revealed that what is around your feet is more likely to be lethal than any animal sprawling contentedly in a tree. Our guide's behaviour had me worried – he seemed preoccupied with his feet and he stared at his green wellies constantly. We paused to admire the great trees that soared to dizzying heights supported by massive buttress roots, like gigantic tendons, that gripped the fertile land and formed pockets for pigmies to stand in and glare out at their enemies. The pigmies have been long driven out, we were told. They had been aggressive defenders of their woodland.

As we trudged the footpath, sudden movements would break out in the bushes or branches above us. The guide stopped and pointed. A red river of insects was ahead crossing the path. Ants. Peering down at these single-minded warriors, it was clear there was no stopping them. An unfortunate giant millipede was being efficiently dissected by these marauders.

We stepped over this river. Ugandan Mangabey monkeys had begun a demonstration of gymnastics, general tree-branch flexing, noise, and confusion. They had been literally hanging around like bored adolescents watching our progress through their territory. The guide shouted Ants! Ants! He was right. The ants were now walking *along* the path and I was standing in the middle of their passage. They were ascending my khaki trousers like commandos on a mission and the only thing to do was run. We all ran, and then stood breathing hard. Grace was flicking them off his shirt frantically with a handkerchief. I did likewise and heard the yelps and curses of men being stung. Remember, *when in forest, look at feet!*

The journey to Lake Mburo National Park in the south of the country meant crossing the equator. We did this in a rickety minibus driven by a fasting Muslim whose driving was insane but brilliant – it had to be. The minibus broke down four times on the way back – a tale for another time.

The equator is marked by a yellow line crossing the road, a gift shop, and a strange monument that you can stand on (I bumped my head) with one leg in the northern and one in the southern hemisphere. Heard the one about water going down a plughole? In the northern hemisphere it swirls in a clockwise direction as it drains out (try it yourself). But in the southern hemisphere it goes down in an anticlockwise direction. It's true. A young man demonstrated this extraordinary effect by marching us twenty metres each side of the equator. And on the equator? Correct. It does not swirl at all but goes straight down the plughole! We stood there in our sunhats and watched this remarkable demonstration with amazement.

In the park itself we saw impala, more impala, yet more impala and zebras by the score. How did zebras ever evolve to be the way they are? Fat, stripy horses kicking up dust storms. Zebras belong really in a Mel Brooks western. They enter stage left with a thunder of hooves then suddenly slam on the brakes. As the dust clears, they stand posing coyly for the camera with their silly manes and tilted hind hooves. A few lens-clicks and they are off stage right with the same relentless enthusiasm searching for a new audience.

We had to stay in the minibus, as walking about was clearly unwise – we would be targets for the six species of death-dealing snakes that share this expanse of grasses and contorted trees. The key to success in the bush for some animals is clearly speed. Families of black wild boar suddenly charge out like motorcycles and are capable of toppling a mere man, even the smallest of these creatures dash about at amazing velocity on tiny motorised little legs.

Warthogs are bigger and more sedate, grazing in happy families, oblivious to the exertions of more frenetic species. They potter about, like aged Victorian gentleman on all fours, searching for the port.

If you are bigger, or better still, huge, you can be self-indulgent and aggressive to anything that moves and have no fear. Like the water buffalo up to his enormous neck in the water hole. Head as big as a Range Rover with huge horns on the sides of his head coiled like the elements on a giant's electric cooker.

Twilight at Lake Mburo is at once serene and deadly. Down by the lake a crocodile slid away under the surface like a nuclear submarine on manoeuvres. In the twilight we could hear the honking of hippos as the last birds curved through the clear air. The menace of the approaching night made us head for the shimmering lights of the local town for fuel and comfort.

Dinner with the Bishop

The Chair of Governors of Ndeeba had just been proclaimed Bishop Elect. Mike and I were invited to dine with him on Wednesday night and, expecting a dry evening, we went to the bar early to wet our whistle before what we imagined might be an occasion of intolerable virtue. At the very moment of decanting a couple of Nile Specials into some tankards, a waiter hurried over to us. "Ah, Mike and John. I'm afraid the Bishop is here." He stifled a grin. Mike took an irreverent swig. So did I. What to do? Delegate!

"Mike. Go and tell him we won't be long." Mike departed. Downing the ice-cold beer, I looked at the waiter who was joking with the barmaid. "John, you're not happy. Don't worry, we stay open all night for you." I grinned back in appreciation – obviously, Mike and I were acquiring a reputation.

I arrived in the reception area to find Mike and the Bishop smiling pleasantly and holding hands. It was a bizarre sight. Handshakes in Uganda can be prolonged, and the Bishop seemed always to hold your hand affectionately for a little too long. He smiled down from his six feet eight inches, immaculate dark suit, and dog collar, in enthusiastic welcome and extended a hand – his left. I shook it. Now he was holding us both by the hand and ushering us out like children to a battered land rover.

Mike headed for the backseat – perhaps he suspected what a completely barmy driver the Bishop was. But he had a minor fright when he encountered William – a tiny little weasel of a man tucked in the gloom in the corner. "William looks after me," explained the Bishop.

We went on a madcap jolting ride up a rutted lane, swerving off into what appeared to be somebody's garden. Through hedges, plantations, bucking and bumping across pitted tracks, I was surprised we didn't pick up a day's washing on our travels. The bishop peered over the steering wheel through thick glasses, thoroughly enjoying every moment, while William pogoed on the back seat and Mike tried to avoid sliding across the shiny leather upholstery and crushing him. Eventually the lights of a bungalow swung into view and we slid to a stop in a shaft of yellow light. The prayer I muttered during the journey was not to be the last that evening.

The Bishop's serene and exquisitely polite wife greeted us in the doorway, and we were introduced to the kind of angelic children you would give your right arm to teach. In their very plain bungalow, we were given a lesson in hospitality and manners, and treated to a meal of subtle curries, steamed chicken, mashed plantain (*maketi*), sweet potatoes, exotic rice dishes and a sensational purple sauce made from gin nuts. Trays of delectable and luscious fruits descended. This was a meal that no wine could complement, and it was accompanied by jugs of exotic fruit juices.

As the family then spoke together in English (for our benefit) about moral and political issues, I reflected guiltily on how impoverished our microwave chips and TV-dinner culture has left us. All the lost opportunities to say the things you need to say, right or wrong, and not run to your computerised virtual world bedroom, and pour out your angst by email to some poor sod in Peru who happens to be in the chatroom at the time. Oh, dear. We have so much to learn.

Suddenly, we returned to the front room and settled on sofas. The Bishop opened an ornate bible, and read the section Exodus 12, v1-30 on the Passover. Everyone listened attentively and the whole family was visibly affected by the seeming incarnation of the Holy Spirit in their front room. There was a sense of awe at the power of God moving across the land, culling the unbelievers like hapless cattle. In the intense atmosphere, I could sense that power invading my sense of self.

Then a discussion began. *Did I like roast meat*, the Bishop asked? What did he mean? I suspected this was code for "Do you want to burn in hell?" I could say nothing. The happy atmosphere had changed instantly, and there seemed a sudden dark, ominous side to faith. Everyone knelt and prayed – Willie was prostrate across an armchair. For me, I concentrated hard, resisting the awe I was meant to feel, searching for the merciful and forgiving image of Jesus in all this. But he wasn't in that room. So, what was? *Dear Lord, get us out of here!*

After the prayers, the sense of oppression lifted. The youngest adopted daughter was still kneeling, her hands trembling, breathless in adoration[2]. I knelt down to speak to her. She looked up adoringly as if bald fat old me was the Lord made flesh. "Hey, come on. Talk to me." Her lip trembled and a quivering hand touched my arm. "It's OK, stand up. It's OK. Talk to me. Say something." Her lips moved. I moved my head closer to listen. Just an inaudible murmur beneath those fearful, awe-struck eyes. "Talk to me, it's OK." Still nothing. I stood up.

Back at the hotel, over a Nile Special, I wondered – and still do – about the morality of conjuring up such images of religious power and allowing them to invade young minds, without analysis. What icons do we have? Have the PR men invaded our minds as deeply? Inured in wet liberal scepticism and woolly notions of freedom of the individual. But the use of fear and fantasy to sway the minds of young people, especially in the hands of powerfully placed and charismatic social leaders is – it seems to me – something to be resisted on every level.

Think of the work our clergy try to do in a society where there are freedoms that a significant minority cannot handle. In Uganda, tending the human flock, teaching the values of freedom, doing God's work on a pushbike is a duty of priests and families. Grace's aunt, a saintly woman who runs a grocery shop in his neighbourhood, put her hand on my shoulder and said, "Are you a Christian?" I nodded slowly, but was I? And whose God was she discussing? "Good. Then we are rowing the same boat." She smiled. *But whose boat?* I wondered.

---

[2] Wordsworth. 'The holy time is quiet as a Nun
Breathless with adoration'

Ndeeba School

We were to pay our final visit to Ndeeba School. In the preceding days, we had taught, played, dined, and laughed with the children and their dedicated staff. As we ambled past children – in their immaculate uniforms – walking to their primary schools, they would smile broadly, point at us and say *mzungu* – a greeting meaning visitor or tourist. At Ndeeba, some children would walk five miles to school each day – others from further away would stay all week, sleeping in the simple bunkhouse. The contrast with the pampered and lazy British lifestyle could not be starker. I tried to explain about the fact that some British children truanted from school – and received disbelieving stares.

One morning, I taught a lesson in English to a class of ninety teenagers. There was one textbook and a chalkboard. My efforts were received with rapt attention and complete silence. No one wanted to miss a thing and I was sure they were writing down every word I said – even conversational stuff like "Good morning!" and "Is it always this hot?" Ninety pairs of young eyes and ears, hanging on my every word. Rare indeed. Teaching and working with these wonderful young people was pure joy.

Before we arrived at the school for the final time, Grace had asked me to talk to the children about Aids. "What do you want me to say?"

"Tell them, if they do not use contraception they will die, they just won't be here to enjoy their future." Grace is quite emotional about this. "John, please remember. I am one of only three surviving children from a family of twelve." I had several conversations with Ida Namugambe during the visit. The epitome of calmness and perception, Ndeeba's head girl had spoken simply and earnestly about how the Aids issue was being mishandled. "We need you to speak about it, sir."

Can there be a better reason for speaking out? The Ugandan churches, for all their might and power, simply advocate abstinence. To me this is unforgivable, and deeply immoral, and to this day the world's faiths fail to recognise that men are the masters of their world and their souls and must bear the responsibility for taking action to prevent disease and disaster. It matters not to me if you have faith or no faith – you can still contract Aids and other STDs if you do not take precautions. Those whose mission is *not* to preach get this and get on with the job of teaching the young people the truth. While the senior clergy seem strangely content to be ignored.

Museveni's government is working hard through the controlled media to get the message across – the radio broadcasts and teaching materials pull no punches, but some teachers are reluctant to use them.

Mike and I are seated like royalty behind heavy oak tables with spotless tablecloths. The school choir sings to us about the partnership between our two schools bringing hope for the future. Then a group of female folk dancers perform before the table, their men pounding handmade drums. The women wear bright costumes with a kind of tufted goatskin apron across their posteriors. They danced across in front of us in a rather tantalising fashion, and I wondered what the missionaries would have made of this rhythmic flaunting of the female form right in front of their noses.

An address from the Head in Bugandan, then my turn. Saying the right things is easy but talking about Aids in another country less so. In the end I used Grace's words to maximum effect. I was fulsome with praise about their beautiful school and their sublime country. The children listened and nodded. It was silent. Now I had to speak out.

"I have a friend," I said. "He is only twenty-five years old. He has been to university; he was an athlete, and he is a teacher. He plays the piano. He loves life. But now the only songs he sings are of despair and loneliness as he watches his life slip away. Aids is killing him, slowly and without mercy. His parents weep as their beautiful son is reduced and worn down by a disease which is destroying his immune system. He suffers pain, he is constantly tired, he has mouth ulcers. He walks unsteadily and experiences anxiety and depression. And why? It was because he had sexual intercourse with an infected person. They did *not* use a condom."

At this point, I notice one of the dancers beginning to cry. The children huddle together as if in a sudden storm. Then I catch the haunted gaze of one of the teachers – a slender young man in a suit too large for him. Grace tells me later that this young teacher has HIV.

I look back at the children and catch Ida's gaze. "Will that be you? Or you, or perhaps you?" casting my glance along the rows of young faces. "Or will you decide to take responsibility for your actions, take control of your life, a control that God has given you and expects you to use?" The children are all staring at me, gripped. More adults are sobbing quietly.

"If people tell you not to use contraception, they are wrong. Do not listen to them. Instead, live. Live and watch your wonderful country blossom in what will be the century of Africa." They all clapped. I felt deeply moved by their sincerity and humility. But I also saw their innocence and vulnerability. I felt Grace's hand on my shoulder. "Thank you, my friend. You have just saved many lives." He gave me a bear hug. Then Lebison slowly and gravely shook my hand. "The children will never forget you."

The clapping had ceased, and the drums restarted. Then more dancing, the students danced, then, *what the hell*, Mike and I danced for all we were worth, goatskins strapped to our ample rears, we danced till we dropped.

Afterwards, we stood in the sun. We shook hands with all the dancers. A woman kissed me on the check. "Thank you," she breathed. The school staff came over and we shook hands and embraced. There was a lump in my throat the size of a jackfruit.

Of course, there were important curriculum links between the students of our two schools in art, English and geography. A rich harvest of photos, video clips and children's work would deepen our A Level students' understanding of tropical rain forests and environmental issues. Everyone in Uganda, it seems, can make an ornate chair, weave beautiful baskets, build a house, make clothes, create jewellery, and paint pictures – how they can paint their homes, people, animals, in rich vivid colours, and produce delectable abstract art and sculpture. Empty the Tate Modern of all its pseudo-Euro metal and stone abstract pop dross trash of unmade beds and exploding pianos and fill its vast spaces to the brim with ebullient African art that does not need to explain itself. Ndeeba's students can turn a piece of backcloth – made from dried tree bark – into a beautiful landscape painting with spell-binding splashes of colour in a trice while you are still nibbling the pencil.

In an age of temporary enthusiasms, this new love affair between this middle-class Englishman and vibrant Africa will last. For staff development, forget courses in airheaded management-speak and motivational gurus. Many of our staff and students will go there. I learned more in a week than I can give Ndeeba in a lifetime, that's for sure.

Grace and Departure

Grace and Irene take us to a nightclub in Kampala. The Afrigo band play delicate rhythmic Santana with uniquely African guitar trails and riffs. The successful twenty-somethings in shiny suits and little black numbers shake and shimmy, their heads bobbing like corks on a wave of sound. Grace asks if I want to dance – remember Grace is male and Irene is watching. Men dancing with men. What to do? When in Rome … Okay.

Presently I realise there is a group of men also dancing with us. One bewhiskered octogenarian with huge braces, smile a piano keyboard, and energy to burn, *hey baby*. *RrrrrrRock on, man*, as he raises each big leg in turn, arms pumping and fingers as big as plantains waggling in ecstatic rhythm. *Ooh, yeah, baby, one time now!* There are three other large men in blue suits in our group, *yo, yo yeahhhhh! Hey, hey, baby.* Something odd about his face, *yeah, rock ON, one time,* is that rouge and eyeshadow? And that bulge, *baby, wotyoudoin'man*?

Grace tells me afterwards, "You know who the old guy is? That's George."

"George?"

"Government minister."

"Oh, ah. The others?"

"The others were his bodyguards."

"And the bulge?"

"Guns."

Gulp!

In departing, some further snapshots. Grace drove us to Entebbe International Airport. At a junction, a girl with long slim legs and almost wearing a sparkly pink dress stood boldly by our car, fixing us with a pouting stare. "Very dangerous people," Grace murmured. "They wait for you by the airport. She will go with you to your hotel room, strip you naked, then use chloroform and rob you. She will phone her friends and they will leave you naked in the park." I gaped and dimly wondered where I could safely hide my Egg Visa card in such a situation.

As we drove into the airport entrance, a slim young man in a vast trench coat stepped out of a booth marked SECURITY and waved us down. He saw Mike and me sitting in the back and asked nervously, "Have you got any guns?"

"No," said Grace.

He thought for a moment and then said, "Are you sure?"

I confess to being completely flummoxed by this and wondering if someone had slipped a rocket-propelled grenade launcher and a few rounds of ammo in with my underwear.

"Yes," said Grace.

"OK, you can go in."

We could have driven in with a boot load of grenades and M60 machine guns, committed some horrendous massacre and given the guard a tip for his pains on the way out. Mind you, looking at it from his angle, with just a trench coat for authority, if a car with five large men draws up, I'm not sure it would be wise to press the point for fear of ending up like a human teabag. The comedy of all this was completely lost on our hosts who just continued chatting cheerfully as they drove round to the terminal.

We sat with our suitcases on a hard bench. Grace and Lebison sat with us; for them it was an essential courtesy to stay with one's guests until the call for boarding was made. Our suitcases were now bulging with gifts and had even crammed some of the fabulous fruit into our bags. As we walked out on to the tarmac, we gave the African sky – bejewelled with stars – one last look. We made a silent vow to return.

Can anything sum up the country? At the Wildlife Park near Entebbe, having walked past two contented and loafing lions, obviously post-lunch, lounging behind some chicken wire, I came upon a water buffalo. But this creature was a pale imitation of the proud monster of the Mburo water hole. He stared balefully from his patch of field with bewildered eyes as if seeking reassurance and wondering about the future.

* * *

That was all in 2001. Now it is Easter 2020 and Ida has sent me a Facebook message. She has found some photos from our visit. The memories are rich and heart-warming. But suddenly, I am recalling that sad water buffalo at Entebbe zoo from the midst of our Covid-19 lockdown. Like him, I gaze blankly through the window of my personal 'zoo'.

Think I know how he felt.

SWING YOUR SHAOBANG

Revealed! The true origins of the game described by G.K. Chesterton as "An expensive way of playing marbles."

I can announce it now. There is a menace to this world greater than global warming, the arms race, terrorism, or even suddenly finding that the taxman has left all our personal data in the loo at Paddington station. I'm talking about golf. This infernal game is taking over the world and is part of a wider conspiracy by the Scottish and the inscrutable Chinese to drive us all barmy. It comes as no surprise.

You can go on a golfing holiday in Vietnam these days. No shortage of bunkers there. Can't wait to tee off at the Agent Orange Golf and Country Club and pop in to the B52 Disco and Bar for a couple of bevvies. According to Professor Ling Hongling of Lanzhou University, the Chinese were playing golf a thousand years ago. Perhaps some of them are still out there, trapped even now in a deep bunker on the dog-leg 13th. He says he has found a reference to a game called *Chuiwan* – Chui meaning to hit, and *wan* meaning ball. Players used ten clubs, including a *cuanbang*, equivalent to a driver today, and a *shaobang*, A3 wood or spoon. Royalty inlaid their clubs with jade, edged them with gold and decorated the shafts elaborately. So, when I play next time, it's out with the old three wood and in with the *shaobang*!

A description of the sport, written during the Song Dynasty (AD960-1279) has been found in a volume called the Dongxuan Records. Professor Ling says the book refers to a Chinese magistrate instructing his daughter to "dig goals in the ground so that he might drive a ball into them with a purposely crafted stick". Golf "clearly originated in China", he said. So how did it reach Europe and particularly Scotland? Well, the good professor says that Mongolian travellers took the game to Europe. They must have stopped off for a knees-up at the Caledonian brewery in Edinburgh. And there it all began.

The Scots, it seemed, got the wrong end of the *shaobang* and goals became holes, and before you could say "William McGonagall", the game was being played by kilted, stick-waving Highlanders across the land. Scottish deer suddenly faced a new hazard in addition to dogs and guns – the Laird's terminal slice off the first tee. Now this highly addictive sport is played around the world, and vast tracts of verdant countryside are being populated by men and women dressed in clothes bought from *ludicrous.com* and pulling little handcarts. It was well described by the American journalist James Reston as "a plague invented by the Calvinistic Scots as a punishment for man's sins".

I caught this disease fifteen years ago. My daughter bought me some golf lessons in a failed attempt to keep me out of the pub. I joined the delightful Bigbury Golf Club – with its emerald fairways and immaculate greens – and I have been shifting turf and terrifying wildlife ever since. It is a game played by gentlemen and ladies at Bigbury but in other parts of the world they have a quite different concept of the word *gentleman*.

In New Zealand, for example, I turned up for a game at the Avondale Golf Club. "Yis! we can find you a *geem*. It's *gintlemin's* day!" Clearly, golf was the real motivation behind the British Empire's smash and grab raid on the Land of the Long White Cloud. 170 years ago, a British gunboat showed up and persuaded the Maori people to sign a treaty. It was very fair. The copy written in Maori said, "You have a very nice country, and we would like to share it with you and live in peace and harmony and learn your culture. We also agree that we don't like the French, do we?"

The copy written in English said, "We agree that we can have your country and build golf courses on it and fill it with five million sheep. And you won't mind because we will allow you to carry on living in your, sorry, *our,* country. And you can become British citizens. How about that! Oh, yes, and we also agree that we don't like the French." As it turns out the small number of French and German colonists who had already arrived there decided to become British as well! Marvellous!

And so it is that when you sit in the clubhouse or go to a leisure centre or supermarket, the Kiwis talk endlessly about their ancestors, a great aunt in Yeovil or their gay cousin in Ilfracombe. Armed with this knowledge I pondered my situation at Avondale Golf Club. "Which part of England are you from?" said the golf pro.

"Oh Devon."

"Oh, what a boomer! My old mum was from Exeter (pronounced *Ixiter*). Small world, isn't it?"

The pro introduced me to Rod, Tony, and Neville. "These guys will give you a game." Which they did. The dress code was different – jeans and trainers – and, what gentleman's day really meant was that just men played. And they spent the time before the game drinking beer and swearing, playing the game and swearing, and then drinking more beer and swearing. When my daughter arrived to pick me up after the game, the whole clubhouse went silent as a hundred pairs of eyes clocked her relaxed stroll to my table; they were probably wondering what on earth I had done to merit a visit from a tall blonde. "Don't worry," I said in response to her quizzical look. "They are more English than I will ever be!"

But I really enjoyed the golf. The blokes cussed and blinded out of earshot of their tidy wives. I really couldn't keep up with the sheer volume of epithets as we hacked and thrashed our way around the course. When we arrived at the 14th tee, Neville decided to ask what I did for a living. "Oh well, I'm in education," I said airily.

"Oh Jeez! You're not a naffing headmaster, are you?"

"Well, erm yes," I stammered, teeing up my ball and then delivering an appalling drive that soared into a gumtree. A huge bird flapped up into the dry air. We carried on playing, And I realised that suddenly the swearing had stopped – we had moved from West Ham to Wimbledon. Until the 17th when I produced a tee shot that took two feet off a sapling. ****** I shouted, and they reverted to 'Kiwi Bloke-Speak' once again.

So, you can see the environmental and cultural mayhem that has been caused by Chuiwan. I really didn't realise how important the surroundings are to an enjoyment of the game. I can remember enjoying cricket most when we played on some of the beautiful grounds across the South of England particularly in Devon and Cornwall – Flete House being a particular favourite, where you had to avoid being trampled to death by point-to-point horses on your way out to bat.

The golf course at Bigbury is particularly striking. There is so much light, sky, and space that it makes simply walking around the course a spectacular joy. As you walk, one cannot help but be amazed by the sheer abundance and plentifulness of wildlife, fauna and flora that spreads across a romantic landscape of elegant curving hills, quiet and secluded valleys, and beyond all that we have the ever-rolling ocean. The sight of the island, with its art deco hotel and ancient pub, truly a jewel set in a sylvan sea. We also have the gentle curves of the River Avon, a rich and teeming artery bringing life to one of the most beautiful valleys in South Devon – a truly breath-taking landscape to behold.

So, how on earth did The Donald - that course, orange-faced Disney villain, aged Dennis the Menace impersonator and egomaniac who now inhabits the White House. ever connect with golf? The plain truth is that while The Donald may be laughable, he has never once said anything wry, witty, or even faintly amusing – not once, ever. He only crows and jeers. And golf is funny, comedy gold. Slapstick of the highest order. Like the friend who was standing in the bunker and suddenly started slapping himself, then dropped his club and ran dementedly across the fairway – he had disturbed a wasps' nest. Or the octogenarian whose electric golf trolley developed a mind of its own, and went speeding across the fairway, finally wedging itself in the fence and tipping the golf clubs into the neighbouring garden.

Mark Twain remarked, "Golf is a good walk spoiled." But I'll leave the last word to our own H. G. Wells, which may explain the POTUS's involvement. "The uglier a man's legs are, the better he plays golf. It's almost a law."

Chris Simes

Author of The Kingdom Chronicles

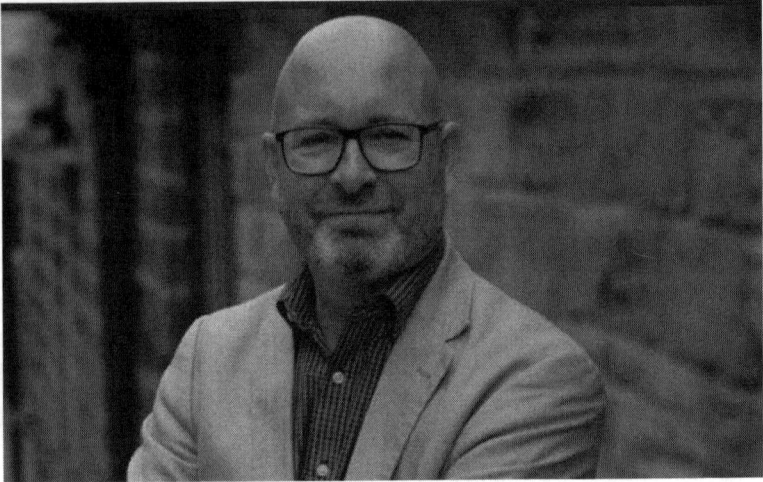

Chris lives with his partner, Lee, in Holmfirth in West
Yorkshire, home of *Last of the Summer Wine*. When he's not
sliding down a hill in a bathtub, Chris is managing director of
an international education company that uses theatre and film
as a learning tool. Because of this, Chris has always written
professionally for work, but never for fun. Writing fantasy has
become a welcome diversion from a growing business, and he
grabs quiet moments when he can to write *The Kingdom
Chronicles*. This might make the book one of the slowest ever
written! Thankfully, the pace is picking up and he's delighted
to finally share a taster of the book for others to enjoy.

THE KINGDOM CHRONICLES

by Chris Simes

Chapter 1: Zurinska

My dearest Lady, I fear we are lost. I have played every move on the board and there is only one left. That is for me to sacrifice my own position to save the lives of my people. If I admit to my culpability in the matter of the rebellion, then I may keep our finest supporters hidden in shadow and the last hope of our people alive. The kingdom now stands firmly in the hands of the Haskans and their mentor. The once peaceable arrangement between our peoples has been eroded over a century and my family ignored your warnings as the tendrils of darkness penetrated every part of our society. I realised too late to pull up the drawbridge and relied on petty schemes and subterfuge to delay the inevitable coup.

As Queen, my only hope is that by accepting exile I can win time for you – great lady – and nameless others to plan, build your strength and await his coming. My father did not believe your warnings, or your message of hope. But I believe. Maybe because it is all I have to cling to. I hope it is because everything you foretold has taken place in this land and I have no reason to doubt you.

I suspect this will be my last communication. Exile is likely a bottomless pit in Haska or a quiet death once I cross the border. But it matters not. Look after my children. My son is weak and has fallen under Eldouine's spell. He will be a poor ruler in my absence. But my daughter. Oh, my daughter. It wasn't too late for me to impart something of our plight to her and infuse her with a glorious loathing for our oppressors combined with a penchant for mischief that might chink Haskan armour enough for light to shine through. Keep an eye on her as she grows. I know you will do right by her when the time comes.

As for the foretelling of a Dransek boy born to release us from these chains, my scholars can reveal little to aid our search, but search we do with immaculate records of birthings in the Kingdom. But I fear this only serves Eldouine's desires as much as it does ours.

My lady, we deserve none of what you have given my family, and my Kingdom. Continue our struggle. I hear them coming for me. The bird likes fennel seeds. He is a good servant.

Queen Theralda Laskofa of Padra

Chapter 2

Fog crept slowly across the plains towards Zurinska. The city seemed to shrink from its towering position overlooking the Sea of the Dawn. She looked up from under her dripping hood, and the last shaft of moonlight caught her white, crinkled skin as she shuffled towards the city, through the knee-high grasses and thistles. Shrouded in a black cloak, and with nothing but a knobbly staff in her hand, she pushed on. The Zhargs had been loosed. She didn't want her long trek to come to an abrupt and worthless end. The Dransek, or "Mother" to those who knew of her, pondered on the next challenge of her exhausting journey. How to get through the gates after dark?

She knew it was her own fault. Her body was tired, tired of a long life. That's why she was late. She quietly cursed her aching limbs for risking the end of her final quest. To be left outside the city would risk being torn apart by hungry

Zhargs, stinking of rotten flesh, and searching for anything to fill their starved bellies. The city lights were twinkling behind the massive, spiked walls that kept people in and Zhargs out. She smelt warm bread, soups, and roasted meats, and decided that no matter what happened at the gate, or in the city, she would have one last meal.

The little figure became even more hunched as she made her way up to the great edifice of the gates of Zurinska. Forbidding black iron had replaced the ivory-coloured gates, decorated with coloured glass, that had stood there on her last visit. That was a long time ago. A small hatch opened, and a helmed head appeared, with large, darting, clever eyes, looking her up and down, then into the fog.

"What time do you think it is?" he asked in a sarcastic drawl.

"Time I got inside those big gates of yours, dear boy," came the answer from this now ancient looking woman, seeming barely to be able to move.

"The Zhargs are loose: you should be dead woman."

"I must be lucky. One day I won't but with my sons killed in the last war I have to earn my keep. I can't rush back inside when the bell tolls like you young ones."

"Too late. My orders are that I cannot let anyone through after dark. Besides, a few morsels for the Zhargs will keep them fit for tomorrow's hunt. Not that they'll get much sustenance from you!" She heard barked laughter from behind the gate.

"Oh dear, Garos will be most upset if I don't heat his water for his bath." The laughing stopped.

"Garos, you say? Garos of the Dread Guard?" The guard was nervous now.

"Why yes dear. Rather fond of me, he is. I've served his family my whole life. He's quite an important man you know, dear. Something to do with city defence if I remember rightly. Are you his friend?" It was the easiest trick in the book. No need for more extreme measures.

177

"Not …friend exactly. Wait there." There was a hushed conversation behind the hatch. A howl came out of nowhere. The Zhargs were getting close. There came the grating of turning locks, and a creak as a small door within the gate slowly opened. "Through here, woman. Quickly, and don't tell anyone we let you in."

'You are a fair and honest lad. How can I repay you?' she said as she shuffled through. The guards, all nearly twice her height, were too busy pushing the door to and turning the locks tight on the door. They weren't taking any chances tonight.

She looked back at the Haskan guards. They were tall, muscular, and covered head to foot in tight-fitting black, spiked armour that shaped each Haskan almost into a uniform physique. As they turned back to watch duty, she noticed the snouts that were larger than an average Padran nose, the immensely powerful jaws, and the wide, hunter's eyes. Their mouths were also wide, with razor sharp teeth. Almost animal rather than human. A stronger, more powerful race, a 'pure' race. Bred to hear, see, and smell more than a simple Padran. They moved like panthers, jumped great distances, and could climb like leopards. Bred to hunt, to kill, to enslave Padra and its people.

Then a thought struck her. Something was out of place! *Haskans guarding their own city?* Far too menial a task, surely? Her suspicions were correct. She wasn't the only one who had sensed it. *He* knew something was afoot too. She had less time than she thought.

The Dransek turned a corner, and was pleased to resume her normal stature, which was slightly less stooped and regal in bearing. She moved as swiftly as she could through the quiet streets, watching for any signs of anything unusual, but all was quiet. The odd Padran tradesman was packing up his cart, and a few raggedy children gaggled at the entrance to a cosy house. The cobbled streets were more worn, chipped, and crooked, less well kept than before, but she still marvelled at the aged beauty and graceful architecture of the larger buildings as she moved towards the centre of the old town, which rose like a phoenix from the lower lying living quarters of the Padran population. She remembered when Zurinska was once a free city. At this time of night there had been jugglers, dancers, musicians and magicians, plying their trade to the delight of adults and children alike. The streets had been fragrant with exotic foods and people nattered, laughed, and sang. In these dark times for Padrans it was quiet, nervous, and suspicious. No one stayed out after dark.

***

Her destination was at hand. She looked to either side from beneath the folds of her hood, and wearily crept down a narrow alley, almost imperceptible between the dark shadows of ancient wooden dwellings. She turned the handle on an old timber door that had one small torch above it and a faded sign. Barely noticeable as an establishment. As the old lady stepped through the ancient doorway she breathed in the smell of roasted game, strong beer, and fragrant smoking leaves. Keeping her hood up, she quietly made her way to the serving hatch and patiently waited for one of the few patrons to be served. It was a small but well-kept tavern, with a roaring fire at each end, and faded padded chairs and benches. She was looking forward to making herself comfortable.

A dark haired, bearded man was serving. He was polite and friendly, seeming to know everyone in his inn, making calm conversation, inquiring after someone's wife or child but keeping himself to himself. He looked simple almost. Just breeches and a tired woollen shirt, with patches on the elbows. He finished serving and looked over to the Dransek. His eyes widened for only a second, as he turned and reached for a tankard and started pouring from his heavy jug of ale. She approached the bar and simply said, "I know it's late, but do you have a room for the night?"

"Have you travelled far?" His voice was gentle and soft.

"Oh, only from Ravenshead, but at my age it is quite a journey."

"Then you'd better take a seat by my warm fire ... my dearest Mother." He named her under his breath so no one else could hear, smiling to her. As she turned towards the fire, she thought she caught him wipe his eyes. She settled by the fire, and took out her short pipe, and folded into it a couple of leaves, and took a long pull and a sip of her beer. Closing her eyes for a moment, she thought to herself, *I've made it to Zurinska. Soon I can rest forever.*

The Dransek felt his presence at her side, after the last of the drinking men had pottered out into the night. Haldarin put down a tankard for himself and a rabbit stew for her. They didn't speak for some time. She took small spoonfuls of stew whilst he drank, both staring into the fire. It was enough just to sit together, for the first time in over two score years. For those long lived, words didn't need to be rushed.

"It's strange, you know," said Haldarin. "I was in the pantry last week, roasting the game, when I heard a tapping on the window." There was mischief in his eyes, as he turned to her.

"My, what was it?" she asked as her faced cracked into a wicked smile and she let out a tinkle of laughter.

"Well, it turned out to be a bird, a raven in fact. Now, I don't like those big black things at the best of times, but this one, well, he seemed most keen to get my attention. I let him in, and he sat on my shoulder for a while, as if to get his bearings. Then I noticed his beak. It had some sort of gem in it. A diamond, if I am not mistaken. Very odd, as they are only found in the White Mountains. The White Mountains are far too far away for a raven to have brought it. I took it as a sign. This raven must be special. It had to mean I was going to be getting a special visitor. It is very special to see you again, Mother. I wondered if I ever would." She smiled in return, and then closed her eyes. In a moment, a black raven came fluttering out from the serving hatch and it perched on her shoulder, flicking at her hair with its beak, as if excited to see her.

"Thank you, my dear Haldarin, for caring for him. You appear to be keeping well."

"Yes, in fact too well. I am getting quite a reputation for continued vitality and youthfulness. Which could get troublesome, if people actually stop and think. I wonder whether I have been helped along the way by something magical?"

"Oh Haldarin, your ways delight me!" Another peel of laughter from the old lady, who seemed to be enjoying herself. "I have to make sure at least some of my friends stay on this earth to keep me company!" They both laughed, but then the old lady became saddened and thoughtful. "Or at least long enough to get something done."

Haldarin stopped laughing and watched her closely. "I haven't sensed anything. I've waited and waited here in this tavern, going about my business and keeping an eye on things, but I haven't sensed it. Mind you, I never had much of a talent in sensing. I was the worst in your little class."

"Your talents were other than sensing Haldarin. Without you we would be lost. You've saved many lives and kept our hopes alive." She took off her cloak for the first time and revealed a gleaming white robe that hung loosely off her thin shoulders. The raven perched atop the mantelpiece. Her presence seemed to fill the room. Her bright white hair hung around a face that was aged, but beautiful. She turned to business. "What of the current state of things?" she asked.

Haldarin paused, then slumped. "It goes worse every year. The Haskans are in total control of the city, reducing Padrans to a slave workforce. The agreement of Telling Falls was a sham. Senior Padrans are all dead, and the Queen is in exile, or at least we hope this to be true. The Haskans rule by their laws as they see fit. Taxes go up, people get poorer and more desperate, and then the Padran tradition of respect for each other breaks down. People fight over grain, steal from each other, and whoever is deemed by the Haskans to be at fault either ends up in gaol, or is used for a hunt. Whichever outcome, they end up dead. I and my friends have saved but a few."

The Dransek narrowed her brow, stared into the embers and pulled on her pipe. "For generations have we endured and waited. I wondered if I was wrong all along."

"People today have no hope. They have forgotten what hope is. Their prayers have gone unanswered for too long and now all they hope for is death and a lasting peace."

Haldarin looked sombre. He took the weight of the world on his shoulders and the Dransek new it. She knew his faith was firm, but how long he could live with enduring this savagery without doing something rash was another thing. She knew he needed to get out of Zurinska. "Are things better in the country?" he asked.

"A little in the more remote enclaves, duchies, and baronies. But many reports we receive talk of similar savagery and oppression. Especially in greater Padra where there is the most fertile land for grain, wine, and other such produce. The same in the mining communities to the north as well as any military strongholds.

"Some of our brother and sister races are either wiped out or enslaved in some way that is useful to the Haskans. Pockets of independence spring up then fall. Those farthest afield and with little to offer can live in relative peace, but they still pay taxes, have Haskan raids inflicted on them, and their children get eaten by Zhargs if they venture too far off the beaten track. Padran villages turn on others to raid for food and goods for taxes, whilst other races either flee or fight with others."

She seemed to lose her age, as her anger welled up and Haldarin saw her gleam more brightly. "But it is to change. I have sensed it. There is hope once more."

He knew what was coming. "You have travelled many leagues and risked your life to come here. Indeed, how you achieved that feat amazes me given the Haskan checkpoints and hunts. Even for someone of your rare talents. So I assume your mission is of great importance. It is something I could not do alone?"

"No Haldarin. I am here for one simple purpose. With your help my task will set in motion a chain of events that I believe will overthrow the Haskans and their leaders. He has come. I sense it."

Haldarin suddenly left his chair and knelt in front of her. "What is my duty, Dransek?"

She took his hands and leant towards him. "When I tell you, do not argue. You must listen and try to understand. Your mission is just starting. Mine is nearly at an end."

***

The Haskan guards sat on a wall, ripping flesh off a well-cooked Drakalt, bantering with each other. Swapping stories of their hunts was a typical Haskan conversation amongst the males. "I knew he was in the swamp, the little shrenk, but I wasn't going to let him get away. I wanted him as well as the Zharg for my bounty. He thought I would worry about the animal, but I'm better than that.

"He was under the water, quick thinking, I suppose. I saw the bubbles and slid into the water. I dived as deep as I could and swam up behind him. He had no idea I was there until he saw his own blood rise up. I dragged him slowly onto the bank and looked into his eyes as he slowly died. He deserved it for running away. No one runs away from a Haskan. I used him as bait for the Zharg, it was an easy kill!" His companion's roar of delight echoed across the city.

It was a magnificent view from the palace. Now under the Haskan command, it was the very highest building in Zurinska, sat atop the Zurinska Dome, a natural rock formation that soared into the sky. The views to the east across the city took in the plains, forests, and distant mountains, while to the west lay the harbour, and the vast ocean, that lay still and threatening. The guards sat, taking in the view. Then there was a noise.

"What was that?" said the other Haskan.

"You're nervous tonight. Give those big ears of yours a rest. We're guarding the palace, not fighting the Zoren! I don't know why we have to do it anyway."

"Something about Padrans not being up to the job these days. Filthy creatures. Isn't it time we got back inside and locked up?"

"Let's get some fresh air for a bit longer. It's stuffy inside." Haskans didn't like being confined. "What's that?"

From nowhere, a raven came swooping down on the surprised guards and grabbed their drakalt meat. It ignored their howls of protest and smoothly avoided their swipes and flew up onto the battlements, along from their position. It seemed to be laughing at them. They started after their quarry, reaching for bows and spears, then stopped, sniffing the air. The wind had changed. They turned to see a hooded being smoothly moving towards the door as if floating rather than walking.

"Who goes there!" growled the lead guard, clearly put out at having his dinner taken and a rude interruption. "Don't creep up on a Haskan. You should know better." They moved forward, looming over the figure, weapons drawn. Their nostrils flared, and their eyes widened in anticipation of a confrontation.

"It's a shame," said the Dransek. "I was hoping you'd chase my bird so I wouldn't have to kill you. Damned wind."

"An old woman? The only one who is going to die is you!" Then both guards launched into the air moving many feet across the ground in one bound, bringing their spears down into fresh air. They stopped, baffled, and turned to find the woman standing behind them.

"I had forgotten how small the Haskan brain is, but also how large the ego," came the steely reply from the diminutive figure now standing at the door of the palace.

Drawing swords, the guards moved circumspectly forward this time, almost snarling with rage at being outwitted. Then she removed her cloak, and both were blinded by the shimmering light that flew from it. It blazed out from their position above Zurinska, setting the evening sky ablaze with light as if to alert the whole town of her presence. Her hair shone with white light and her body took on a ghostly, almost transparent hue. Her staff pointed towards one of the guards who immediately flew backwards, over the palace wall, and down the hundred feet to the streets below.

Her voice echoed out across the town with a pure, almost musical quality. "I will let you live Haskan so you may witness the return of the Dransek. For many years we have endured, along with our Padran friends, as you seek to destroy us and our way of life. But we endure, and will endure, long enough to rid Zurinska and Padra of your savagery. I return to signal a new beginning, and to tell all that there is renewed hope." The dark city twinkled into life, as candles were lit and shutters opened. "I, the last Dransek, am here to tell all that I am not the last any longer. A boy has come, a Dransek of immense power. He will overthrow the Haskans forever."

As the quaking Haskan cowered, the palace gate burst into blue flames, and the Dransek stepped back through the fire and vanished, leaving a residue of light shimmering above Zurinska.

The Dransek pulled her cloak around her shivering frame, and leant on her staff, exhausted. Having found a narrow corridor that was in darkness, she rested there in a dark vestibule, for only a few seconds, catching her breath and regaining her composure. It was harder and harder these days to use her powers without feeling drained of life. But there was no time as it wouldn't take long for the Haskans to group, and hunt. More wily pack leaders would know more than a youthful guard, and before she knew it Haskan packs would be bounding through the corridors eager for blood, her blood. There would be no escape from their heightened senses for even a Dransek. No escape. But that was irrelevant. She pushed herself up to her feet with her staff. She had to get to her destination. She must complete the task. The small, cloaked figure swept down the hallway.

***

"Here in the Palace!" roared the Haskakin, the pack leader. He wasn't known for calmness. "And you let her go! What kind of hunter are you?"

"The light blinded me," replied the guard, who had witnessed the Dransek's actions. "I was stunned, it froze me, I couldn't move. She grew larger in front of me, before my very eyes and made the darkness go away. Then she spoke about coming to free the Padrans. The voice carried for miles."

"What else did this thing say?" said the Haskakin, who suddenly went pale. "Think you useless Ragdoon or you will die at my hand now, in this room."

The guard was erect, proud, but sweating profusely and visibly shaking. "Sir," he barked. "It was something about a Dransek. A new Dransek is born. Her voice reached out to the people saying they would overthrow us. I cannot remember it all." The sergeant's eyes widened, and he gripped the hilt of his sword.

"You have said enough!" To the assembled throng, he snarled, "Sound the horns, search this she-creature out. Encircle the palace, and spring the trap! The hunt is on!" Several of those present left the room, and immediately there was a vibration in the building as a Haskan hunting horn sounded, then another. "You, guard. You have failed. You are no Haskan. Fall on your sword."

"But sir, please, let me hunt with the others." The guard was almost crying as he realised his fate. To kill yourself was to accept your failure as a hunter. "Let me die hunting her. Feed me to her!"

"You, hunt the Dransek! Fall on your sword." With an anguished bellow, the guard took out his sword, and thrust it through his torso, roaring the word *Haska* until it became a nothing but a gurgle. The sergeant took a drink from his metal vial. He sat down heavily.

To the remaining Haskans he barked, "Go tell Eldouine of this news. Leave me. Hunt!" After the arched room had emptied, he muttered an oath, then reached for his dagger. His fate would be worse than the guard's if he lived to receive it.

The Dransek breathing became ever more laboured, as she rounded a corner and saw what she had been looking for. Birthing records. No one counted the deaths, only the births. They had good reason, and that was why she was here.

Drawing all her resources together, she who Haldarin called Mother sent from her staff a burst of white energy towards the lock and the door came away. She swiftly entered without looking back. She heard screams of anger and delight from other corridors as the Haskan hunters stalked through the palace in search of her, but suddenly they were quiet. It meant they had picked up her scent or seen signs of her presence in this part of the building.

They would be moving slowly now, in packs, drawing hardly any breath, alive to every sight, sound or smell that gave away their prey's location. Inside the room, she moved silently over to the rows of leather-bound books, each two foot in width, painstakingly notated by Padran scribes every day of their dull, miserable lives. The room, normally a hive of activity, was dark, with shafts of moonlight slicing through the narrow stone arches that were windows.

She knew what she was looking for, and immediately found the station and book she required. Haldarin had always been accurate in his information, and clearly had a well-positioned Padran in the palace to be able to gather such knowledge.

As she leafed through the pages of the book, her raven was already there, atop an open window, quietly awaiting his next role in this adventure. Then she saw it. The freshly quilled lettering spelling a new birth, and a re-birth for Padra. She had been correct! Not that she had ever been in doubt. After memorising the line of carefully written text, she waved a hand and it vanished. Just as the Dransek turned to the raven at the window, a haunting voice spoke out from the doorway. "Mistress of the Dransek. We meet again." Her heart stopped.

"Eldouine. What a pleasant surprise. You really are slowing up in your old age. I thought you would have found me before this." She continued to stare at the raven before finally turning to face her foe.

Eldouine was younger than her in appearance, but in their world time moved at a different pace. He stood with only a rod of iron at his side, in black flowing robes and a mild stoop. Eldouine's features were stark. His slightly crooked neck supported a face with snow-white skin that was almost translucent, stretched over a high forehead with wisps of white hair and a low jaw, which housed a thin lipped, blank expression. His eyes were the most terrifying thing about him. They were set back in dark hollows, and the iris was jet black.

"I can't be everywhere at once, I admit," he spoke slowly and softly, almost a whisper but with a mocking overtone. "But our empire is large, and my services are … unique. Not that I mind, of course, the rewards are enough. Such as seeing you scrabble to overturn the inevitable in your last moments of mortal life, with nothing left but a few magical tricks.

"However, I must admire your ingenuity. I sensed it too, but later than you. Perhaps I have been away from my kind too long. This is of little concern to us. Even without that line of text you have so inconveniently erased, I will do what has been done before, and destroy your pitiful hope when he gives himself away. Your little performance outside the palace meant you would never fulfil your task and see this bastard creature to safety. You always had a penchant for vanity, just like the Padrans, poor things. That's why I prefer simpler people who lack such frailties.

"The strongest always win through wouldn't you say? This will be the last Dransek, I have no doubt. The shining new hope that you and your little band so vainly cling to is making its last stand. As are you my dearest sister. Making your last stand."

The Dransek laughed her silvery words. "Eldouine. Your speech was magnificent as always. Most well thought out, and insightful, but unfortunately you underestimate us. You are right though. This is my last stand. It's time for us to move on Eldouine. We are old and must make way. It is the way of things.

"You think you are more powerful, and you are. But you are just like your Haskan counterparts. The more power you have, the more you crave. In your case I suspect this has to do with not being able to accept the natural way of things. Your own death. I am sure you search for life eternal and use every magical device you can find to sustain it. But, the more power, the less guile. You are evil, Eldouine. That makes you vulnerable."

"Oh but eternal life is far too small an ambition for me, Sister. Your sympathies with Padrans have limited you to Padran logic," spoke Eldouine softly. "For that reason alone, your time has come to be ended."

He raised his rod lightly, as she dropped her cloak and stood shimmering once more in the darkness. His blast of red energy was only countered by her white spell at the last moment. She threw her head back and poured her remaining energy into her magic.

As they duelled and the furniture singed and the books burnt, she sensed his dark power, his dark mind, and the horrors Eldouine had embraced and worshipped. She sensed anger so deep it fuelled his very being. She was fast being overwhelmed by his powers, and desperately tried to bring forth greater white magic. She had never felt weaker and feebler than she did at that moment.

She fell to her knees, drawing her final breaths, just as another figure emerged into her consciousness from a side door. Instantly a dagger flew from its owner's hand an embedded in Eldouine's chest. He stopped his attack and looked down at it, with only a minor stumble.

"A crude device to use against Eldouine," he commented. Both he and the Dransek looked towards the intruder. It was Haldarin. He was bleeding, with ripped clothes, and one arm hung limply at his side. His eyes were wild.

"You will not destroy our Mother!" he bellowed, crazed. The Dransek looked up in shock, and her hopes crashed around her. *You were supposed to follow my instructions. Now we are all lost. You submitted to anger and made my sacrifice worthless.*

Haldarin roared and lumbered towards Eldouine, who merely raised a thin, withered hand and the Dransek watched as her faithful follower dropped to the floor slowly as if hit on the head with a stone. He came to rest as pieces of charred parchment slowly floated to the floor around him. Eldouine pulled the dagger from his own chest, and black bile spilled from the opening. He looked at the Dransek, deep into her eyes and they held that moment for what seemed like minutes but was only seconds. Then he staggered again. "I leave you to my guileless friend's sister." And with that remark, he shimmered and vanished.

She knelt by Haldarin, as the Haskans moved slowly into the room. They entered by every door and window. They came by the dozen, slathering, shrieking, some on all fours like cats, others climbing the walls, gripping the stone with the claw-like feet, all moving as one, closing in on her weak, hunched body, leaning protectively over the lifeless form of Haldarin. She gripped her staff and looked up to the window.

The raven had gone. She closed her eyes for her final journey.

From *The Kingdom Chronicles* by Chris Simes –
Collingwood 2021.

Vanessa J. Chapman

Author of
The Sound of Tea

Vanessa is an English teacher living in East Kent with her partner and her two (practically) grown-up, children. She had at one time fancied herself as a potential writer of books but has settled for the occasional dabble into short story writing. Vanessa has a Master of Arts in Education and after having worked for many years on projects that support students from disadvantaged backgrounds, she eventually took the plunge into teaching in 2018. She thoroughly enjoys her challenging yet rewarding role in a further education college. She is an avid reader, getting through one to two books a week in a range of genres. As well as reading, she likes to unwind by baking and walking in the countryside.

THE SOUND OF TEA

by Vanessa J. Chapman

It was six months before I noticed the gradual disappearance of the teacups. I owned three full tea sets, and a dozen mismatched cups and saucers. It was one of my blue cups with the daisies that went first. We had used that one on the day she came to me. It was part of a complete set, and when I tidied them away, I noticed I was one short, the saucer was still on the draining board but not the cup.

I thought perhaps she had broken it and been too embarrassed to say. I saw no need to make her feel awkward and chose not to mention it the next week when she came. Three weeks later the saucer disappeared, and that's when I knew she was taking them. As I hadn't mentioned the cup, I could hardly now mention the saucer. It was a design that was still available, and I was able to replace the lost cup and saucer without the need to say anything to her.

It was the sound that did it for her, I'm certain it gave her comfort in some way. When tea is poured out of a pot and into a cup it creates a unique sound. A proper teapot with a cup and saucer. It's not the same sound at all when you pour from a kettle into a mug. And the chink of the teaspoon in the cup. Yes, she always responded to those sounds.

She spoke of sitting cross-legged on the carpet under the table as a child while her mother poured the tea, therefore she could not have seen her mother pour it, only heard it. I don't know why she sat under the table, she never said why, only that she did. Each afternoon.

They had cake too. Her mother would pass her a cup and saucer of tea, and a slice of cake under the table, and she would sit, cross-legged, and break off small pieces from the cake, practically crumb by crumb, and savour each tiny pinch.

When the tea was cold enough to drink, she would sip it methodically. She loved how it felt when it slid down her throat. She said it was like silk. Those were her words; that she loved how it felt like silk sliding down her throat. These were her happiest childhood memories she said.

From her vantage point under the table, she could observe her father sip his tea and eat his cake. He sat in a worn upright green armchair on the other side of the room. When he was finished, he would direct his attention to her, gesture towards the cake, and say, "Are you enjoying that, Margaret?" She would nod and smile. She never spoke. Merely nodded and smiled. It's the only thing she ever remembers her father say to her. He wouldn't say it until he had finished his last sip of tea and placed the cup back in the saucer. She knew it was his last sip because he would sigh after it.

You see? It makes sense now. The sounds. Placing his cup back in the saucer, and the sigh, more sounds, sounds that meant he was about to speak to her.

It was seventeen years ago when she first came to me. I had placed a card in the newsagents' window in the village: "House cleaner wanted for woman living alone, one morning a week, light housework duties only." And my contact details. The next morning, she arrived on my doorstep and said: "Hello, I'm Margaret, I'm your new cleaner." Just like that.

She assumed that the job would be hers if she simply turned up. It wasn't arrogance or anything; she was too gentle in nature to be arrogant, it's how she was, that's all. She didn't know how to be any different. I nodded, introduced myself as Jen, and invited her in. And that's how she came to be my cleaner.

She accepted my offer of a cup of tea that morning. I noticed her expression was one of intense pleasure, mixed with mild agitation. I served the tea on a tray. A delicate blue teapot with painted daisies, and matching cups and saucers. In truth, when I'm on my own I have a mug and fill it straight from the kettle, but when I have visitors, it's a teapot with cups and saucers.

The agitation seemed to disappear when she saw the cups. We chatted, but when I poured the tea, she stopped mid-sentence. It's as if she forgot she was even speaking. Her eyes widened as the deep brown earthy tea cascaded into the cups, and the corners of her mouth curled upwards. I could tell she was listening too.

I waited for her to carry on speaking, but she didn't. She stirred her tea and closed her eyes. I realise now it was to listen to the chink of the teaspoon in the cup, but at the time I didn't know what to make of it. We sat and drank in silence, and when we were finished, she said "Shall I start in the kitchen then?" And she did.

The next week she brought cake with her, two slices, and each subsequent week too. She cleaned for an hour and a half. Then I made tea, and we sat and drank tea and ate cake. She would break off little pieces of cake and eat them, pinch by pinch, and when I commented on it one day, the story of her childhood tea and cake under the table emerged.

After the tea and cake, she cleaned for a further two hours, and was done. I was intrigued by the way she drank her tea. She kept each sip in her mouth for several seconds, a wistful air about her while she gazed into the distance, before she swallowed. And in between each sip, the cup was lowered back down on the saucer, only to be lifted back up immediately after. For the sound I expect.

And this is how things continued. For years. Sometimes weeks or months would pass in-between the taking of the teacups. But after a while I kept records. I counted how many cups and saucers in each design I had, and after each of her visits, I counted again. Sometimes I could replace exactly, sometimes not. Funny, I never considered what was in her mind. She must have noticed the cups and saucers she took were replaced. I wonder now what she thought about that.

I grew fond of Margaret over the years. It was a deep friendship of sorts. I looked forward to our regular tea and cake together. The two slices of cake she brought were always homemade. Her mother's recipes, she explained. Nothing but her mother's recipes. "Mother made the very best cakes in the world," she always said.

One day, she hesitated and added that I made tea how her mother had, and I knew this was the greatest compliment she could give.

On a biting November morning, I stoked the fire in the living room while Margaret vacuumed upstairs. I heard a thump, more than heard, felt. I called up to her but received no reply. I found her lying on my bedroom floor, flat on her back, vacuum hose still in hand, skirt half sucked up the end. We hadn't even had our tea yet. Her eyes were open but glazed over.

At first I thought she was dead, but as I moved to her, I was comforted by the rise and fall of her bosom. "Margaret!" I called. "Margaret, can you hear me?" The ambulance arrived swiftly, and they took her away. I would have gone with them, only I noticed her keys on my hall table and knew what I would do. She would need an overnight bag at least, and I would probably be able to find a phone number of a relative, or somebody to contact. To let them know what had happened. The guilty wrench in my gut, however, confirmed I had other reasons for wanting to go to her house.

I had imagined her house to be rather old and dingy, but I was wrong. The entrance hall was bright and modern. Painted perfect white, with a well-polished natural light wood floor. There was a staircase of the same wood on the right, and on the left were two doors. A pleasant smell of jasmine filled the air.

I could see that one of the doors from the entrance hall led to the kitchen, I chose the other. I was aware of a nervous shake in my hand as I pushed the door. I found myself in a large living and dining room, the type which had at one time been two separate rooms, subsequently knocked into one. And that's when I saw them. A wave of cold coursed through me, and I gripped the doorframe to steady myself.

Along the whole length of the far wall, from the living area through into the dining area, stretched glass-fronted cabinets. Six of them, side by side. All the same type. I estimated they covered at least thirty feet in total, and each contained five shelves. Crammed onto the shelves were dozens, no, hundreds of cups and saucers.

At first I thought they were unorganised but as I stepped closer, I saw they were clustered together in groups, and on the lip of the shelf in front of each group was a label with a name. A person's name. And a little description. "Mrs Hemming – likes Mother's fruit cake best." "Susan – favours white cups with roses on like Mother did." "Mr Arnold – says he wishes he had known Mother." I scanned the shelves until I found my name: "Jen – makes tea with love like Mother did."

I read the words three times before my eyes clouded. Tears slid down my cheek and found a path into the corner of my mouth. Here in these cabinets was the teacups' final resting place, and now they were silent. I allowed my tears their freedom while I walked the length of the cabinets and read each label. When I was done, I backed out of the room. Upstairs, I found her bedroom and threw a pair of pyjamas and a change of clothes into a small holdall bag, followed by her toothbrush and paste from the bathroom. And I left the house.

At the hospital I was directed to wait. After ten minutes I was taken through to her. She was conscious and smiled as I walked in. Music came from a radio embedded in the wall behind her. Her smile faded as I placed the bag on her bed. I breathed deep for courage and spoke with feigned jolliness. "So, how are you feeling? Have they said what was wrong?" Margaret's gaze was fixed on the bag.

"You saw, didn't you," she said.

"Yes." I perched myself on the edge of the bed and we sat without speaking through two songs. Margaret was the first to speak.

"I'm not crazy, you know."

"I know."

"I expect a psychiatrist would say that I use tea as a replacement for love. Don't you think a psychiatrist would say something like that?"

"I don't know. Would they be right if they did?"

"No. I do know the difference between tea and love. I just like tea, you know. And cake. And teacups. They make sounds. I like that."

"I know."

"I'm sorry for taking your cups, do you want them back?"

"No, you keep them."

"Are you going to find a new cleaner now?"

"No, I wouldn't be able to trust anyone else."

The humour was not lost on Margaret and we laughed. Some may find it perverse that we should laugh, but then I couldn't expect anyone else to understand. There was no more to be said, and only one thing to be done. I moved up to sit closer to her head and wrapped my arms around her. She wrapped her arms around me and rested her head on my shoulder. We held each other tight for a full four minutes. I know it was four minutes because my wrist was in front of my eyes, and I counted the second hand going around. And then I left.

You might imagine she would have stopped taking my teacups after that. But she didn't. It wasn't arrogance or anything; she was too gentle in nature to be arrogant. It's the way she was, that's all. She didn't know how to be any different.

Gary Maguire

Author of The Guide

Gary Maguire (aka McBar) was born and bred in the Kingdom of Fife. After circumnavigating the country, he came to rest in Devon, where he has been quietly plotting against the nation ever since. He supposedly spends his time between Burgh Island and Tavistock although no one is really sure ... Somewhere along the way he became a national treasure. He is a member of the Bigbury Hobblers, a sect known, despite their adversities, for their peculiar shackling gait. Any local will tell you that if you can't find anything good to say about anyone, you should come and sit next to Gary.

THE GUIDE

By Gary Maguire

John Pepperpool, the Coastguard, had been watching, binoculars trained. He spotted Tom sitting over on the Murrays rocks. John jumped into the Toyota Hilux and drove down the slipway onto the beach.

Tom had been enjoying the early morning sun. Swallows wheeled and darted in the warm morning air. He counted seven of them. Seven for a secret. Or was that magpies? The sun hung in the bluest of blue skies. And what a blue! As near to the shining iridescence of perfection as it could get on this June morning. The unknowability of a summer's morning and what would the day bring? Hopes were as high as that patch of alto cirrus up there.

It was still early. No one around. Low tide, although now just beginning to turn. Tom lay on the beach in his neoprene summer shortie, board by his side, listening to the Roberts radio nestling in the sand. The Blue Nile had segued into Coldplay. Now there was a team: Chris Martin and Nicole Kidman, just like him and Emma, although they had fallen out this morning. Ems wanted him to come with her to Ivybridge but Tom wanted a bit of Bigbury surf. He'd make it up to her tonight.

To his right lay the towering wedding cake of the famous Burgh Island hotel with the little Pilchard Inn nestling, rather like an aged terrier in its shadow. To the left of Tom was the mouth of the Avon, with the shoreside villages of Bantham and Thurlestone beyond. Clouds were beginning to gather over Bantham bottom. A promise of rain somewhere but that didn't mean here; it may develop further north towards Ivybridge or go south into the Channel. Such were the vagaries of the coast.

"Time for rip curl," he murmured.

Tom waved over to the Challaborough side of the beach. Sheila Rode waved back. Sheila was a diamond. Sheila swam every day. Winter and summer. Tom had already zogged up his board that morning so, attaching the leash to his ankle, off he trotted to the mouth of the Avon. Rip curl. The waves looked washy but there was a slight onshore breeze which would help things. One, two, three, he was in. The exhilaration of the water always got him. That first trickle through the wetsuit down his back and he was there, paddling out into the deeper water, through the waves. Bouncing through. Brick wall. Glacier. Brick wall. Glacier. He *loved* this.

Turning back in, he caught a wave – and for a few seconds, was up. Then not! This was the life. He was out again and back in, having caught another wave. Funny how strong that current was underfoot, he thought to himself. Two minutes ago, he could feel sand under his feet. Now he was treading water. The tide was coming in.

He caught another wave and crashed under, swallowing sea water. He was snatched by another surge which disoriented him. He slid under, before remerging. This was not good. Something was wrong. He felt for the seabed, but it wasn't there. The salt water blinded him. Was he out further than he thought? The water was beginning to race over his head, the fast current coming down from the river, tumbled him over. A *washing machine*. He couldn't find his footing! This was not good. He hated to think. He was in trouble. He took on board another mouthful of saline and choked.

The clouds over Bantham darkened.

"Panic and you're dead … don't panic … don't panic!" *Keep the head. Or you're dead.*

A sickening feeling started to grow in his stomach. Was this it? You never knew how it would happen until it did. This was now a situation. Suddenly it was here. No time to do anything. He was struggling. He was churned over again. He lost his board.

Trying not to panic, he knew that he needed to go out with the current and somehow get out of the rip by swimming to the side. This was easier said than done when one was in it. Dangerous waves were all around him. High. There was a lady on the beach, walking her dog. Was that Trish? Was she looking over? Did she see him? He raised his arm, already weakening. Trish, he now realised, was the last thing he would see. The Last Great Stillness. That supreme final, final emotion as we move from one plane to another. Sickness came back to his stomach. The last things went through his head. Randomness. Roly. Ems. The postman. The Fiat, sitting alone in the car park up there. No one returning to it. The fluffy toys in the bathroom. The unopened letter on the kitchen table. The towel, radio and car keys, lying on the beach. All the pathetic things. The waves roared.

"Are you alright mate?" The water roared in his ears now. He was gulping water.

"Are you alright mate?" He could see nothing but spray. He was going down. Something hit his leg.

His board had returned. He clung to it. He could see nothing but waves. He struggled to get on the board. His ears fizzed.

"You OK mate?"

Was he hearing things? A voice. Near. Thank the Lord for the board. Even in this extremis, Tom was beginning to think again.

He got on the board. Someone was there. Someone to his left. Where had he come from? There had been no one else around. There was now someone there.

Tom shouted.

"Help me. In trouble."

"I can see. Stay on your board. Follow me."

"OK." Blindingly and choking, Tom followed this Deus, this Machina, appearing from nowhere. The secret was to get as much of one's weight out of the water and try to skim, like a water beetle, on the surface of the water.

He followed the big guy who went to the right, in the direction of the Murrays rocks.

"You were going the wrong way. We'll get out of it here. I'm Will, by the way."

He could hear things again. He kept skimming and so did Will. Slowly the grip of the sea lessened. He could hardly believe what had just happened.

Will commented. "I was caught in that once. A long time ago. Never again. It teaches you."

"Thanks, Will."

Tom felt like he was more on an even keel. His heart was beginning to rise again. He was out of it, thanks to this guy who had appeared at a point of perverse exactness. He had no doubt that, in a few more minutes, he would have been a goner. People say that drowning is one of the best ways to go but Tom didn't want to find out firsthand. He was eternally grateful for Will's appearance. They both paddled to the rocks and sat together, catching their breath, Tom slowly recovering his poise.

Having recovered enough, Tom turned to Will. Jestingly, he said, "I haven't seen that outfit in Fatface, Will!"

True. Will was wearing a one-piece knitted swimming costume. A woolen affair. Maroon red. The kind of thing seen in old films. Tom had to chuckle. "You look like something out of a Poirot film."

"Didn't know there were any films made," he said falteringly. "I like the books."

They sat in silence. "Got to go," said Will. "Remember to whistle next time."

Will paddled on the board towards the Murrays rocks and disappeared round the back of the island. Tom sat on the rocks, wondering if it had all been something he imagined.

Rain was imminent. Tom swam with his board onto the beach. He saw John Pepperpool's Hilux – lights flashing – on the beach.

"Hi John. I could have done with your help a few minutes ago."

"Sheila Rode phoned me," continued John, "She could see you were in trouble. I came as quickly as I could."

"Thank the Lord Will appeared at the last minute."

"Who's Will?" John asked, curious.

"The guy who was with me. He brought me out of the rip."

John was silent. Then he turned astonished eyes at Tom.

"Look, you got out of that on your own, Tom; there was no one with you. I've been up there at the cafe this last few minutes and you were on your own. So well done. Get home and get yourself sorted. Get yourself a proper board mate. That one looks like it belongs in a surfing museum."

Tom looked. He was holding a plywood board, the type used way back in the thirties. Then it was known as surf riding. A six-foot gun. Tom's own board was lying on the shoreline, just past the Murrays.

The first drops of rain were beginning to fall.

JOHN SIMES

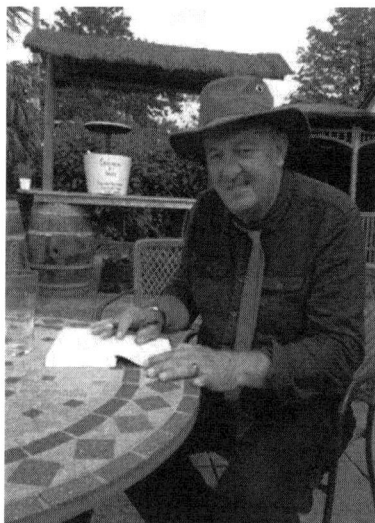

After his career in education, in 2013 John founded Collingwood Publishing & Media Limited. *The Upperthong Thunderbolt* is his first collection of short stories, featuring the places in West Yorkshire, Ringmore, Challaborough and Bigbury in south Devon that he knows and loves.

In 2018, John published his second novel, the surreal comic thriller, A Game of Chess, the sequel to his acclaimed debut *The Dream Factory.* He also edited and published the collection of poetry by Laurence McPartlin *Wake the Stars* (Collingwood 2019). You can find out more about John at www.johnsimes.co.uk or follow him on Twitter: @johnthepoet2010.

The final part of The Dream Factory – *Cape Farewell* – in which Peter and Navinda flee England to escape the Golden Hand – will be published in 2022. Here is the opening.

CAPE FAREWELL

Prologue

You're here again. I understand.

Your need to know is strong. As is mine.

Because we know that The Golden Hand has been withered but not slain. Scotched the snake. Not killed it. It can rejuvenate. It can exist as a blood speck, a mite, a tick that will come to feed while you sleep innocent dreams. Or it will lurk like a parasite on your hard drive and appear as a ghost on the screen. It will have a calm, quietly smiling face. It will have a name like Alexis or Gudrun. It will have sensible blonde hair, styled in a bob – the A-list hairstyle du jour. A soothing mid-Atlantic voice. Cartoon eyes that blink as they photograph your face. It will look and know you. It will study the pictures of your children on the wall. It will note the newspaper you are reading, and the books that line your shelves, and infiltrate your files to find your next holiday.

It will know you in ways that will chill your heart. It will know your biology, your bone marrow type, your weaknesses.

We must resist. But some of us are asleep.

Except you and me. John and Esther – Peter's parents – have returned to work at Caid-a-Ford. Yes, the Caïssa Project.

And Rosencrantz has retreated to a bitter harbour where he plans and schemes.

Gerald has retired to paint his landscapes and look deeply into the heart of things.

But the earth turns. Peter and Navinda have gone to seek the dolphins – those astounding sea jesters – in a place

whose name I dare not breathe. You will know.
Dingwell has a visitor.

Chapter 1

Hookworm

Constable Dave Rabbetts yawned. Seated on the plinth of Dingwell's only granite crucifix, he leaned back, resting his head on the mottled ancient stone, he raised his eyes to the sky. A hawk was carving magnificent lines in the morning sky. *Not a bad life*, thought Dave, who had been tasked with guarding the gates of The Old Rectory in Dingwell, the home of John and Esther Young and their son, Peter.

Dave had watched as the Young's Range Rover had emerged from the new steel security gates, before speeding off up Church Lane towards Greymoor and Caid-a-Ford. The electronic gates had swung slowly shut. But Dave had a key, which meant he was able to show that nice young chap from the Totem Broadband Company into the house. The man had waved a pass at Dave, who carried the man's sleek aluminium attaché case into the kitchen and received ten quid for his trouble.

WPC Yvonne Bull smiled down at Dave as she jogged past him on her morning run. Dave felt a surge of passion as he watched her blond ponytail bobbing; she strode rhythmically, in her white police top and blue shorts. But the lovelorn Dave knew that Yvonne's heart had fallen elsewhere. Ah well. Everyone seemed to have someone but him. Peter Young had gone off travelling Lord knows where with his girlfriend, Navinda. Even the vicar's wife had come back to him – with three kids in tow. Funny business that! Ah well, there was that nice Brenda, the new PCSO. She had smiled at him and stirred a sachet of sugar into his frothy latte. Dave beamed at the memory.

* * *

Kernac was standing in the hall of the Old Rectory. Having installed the Hookworm parasite software on the Youngs' Apple Macs, Kernac pondered the question of where Peter Young and Navinda Eman had gone. Peter had left Queensbridge College and the school's leaky computer system was no longer providing a daily report on Peter's attendance and his sullen reluctance to engage in any academic work - all stoically recorded by Mr. 'Gabby' Root, Peter's long-suffering tutor. Equally, a simple telephone call to the Jannah Academy in Birmingham had elicited the information that Navinda had completed her Baccalaureate – achieving grades of a truly Olympian scale – and was planning to travel. The flustered telephonist at the Academy had kindly put Kernac's call through to Navinda's tutor, Miss Kramer, but Navinda's inspiration and mentor had declined to divulge any information and abruptly ended the conversation. Flora Kramer had then alerted Navinda's family.

Kernac's eyes scanned the photographs lining the staircase in the hall. They were framed in driftwood, decorated with pieces of coloured glass and seashells. Kernac's stance was perfectly upright and military, his grey eyes alert above the aquiline nose, elegant jawline, marble complexion, slim dark eyebrows, and the classic Olympian cheekbones of the master tactician. As he surveyed the pictures, Kernac's finely tuned insight and impeccable logic focused on the more curious of the images. It showed the head of an ape, apparently sculpted by the sea from giant sandstone cliffs. John and Esther were posing in front of the huge, hooded eyes and gorilla lips of the natural sculpture. Inset into the picture was a thumbnail of a young Peter sitting on top of the gorilla's formidable brow. Cape Farewell, murmured Kernac; he realised there were several smaller prints in wooden frames along a shelf. Where would you go to get lost? Where better?

* * *

Yvonne had jogged to the end of Church Lane and paused for breath. She looked down the length of the driveway to The Fossils – the Georgian manor house, enclosed with mock castellations and turrets; it was the exclusive home of the eccentric Miss B. Yvonne smiled, recalling Miss B's spectacular birthday party. She turned and looked back along the lane once more. Constable Dave waved cheerily from the base of the old stone cross. The side gate to The Old Rectory opened. A slender man wearing overalls and a peaked cap emerged and nodded to Dave, who gestured farewell.

But there was something familiar about the man's shape, his gait, his perfectly vertical stance, and rhythmic walk. The man turned and was striding back to the village. Yvonne's heart leapt. She broke into a run. *That bloody fool, Dave.*

"Stop!" she shouted. "Dave! Stop him." The man accelerated into a jog, then a run, and he disappeared around the corner past the church.

Constable Dave made a feeble attempt at pursuit, before standing hands on hips in the middle of the lane. Yvonne came racing towards him. She burst past and sprinted in the direction of the church. A Mercedes turned from the church car park and roared up the hill. Yvonne tried to catch her breath as the car vanished over the summit. Dave arrived at her side, puffing.

"Who was he, Dave? Who was he? Why did you let him in!" Dave was shaken by her anger.

"He was from that company, internet thingy. Here! I got his card." Dave pulled a grey business card from his pocket. Yvonne studied it. "See there. Mr. Lee Berners. Totem Transmissions."

Yvonne gazed up at Dave's kindly, trusting face and curly hair. "Dave, it wasn't a Mr. Berners. And he wasn't from Totem Transmissions."

"Oh, uh! Who was it then?"

"Don't worry your head, Dave. I know who it was. And he was leaving a message."

* * *

Rosencrantz finished his coffee. It was a dark, rich Sumatran coffee, with a touch of bitterness that matched his mood. The Romanesque architecture of Castle Boodlé, and the snow-capped razor's edge of the Dents du Midi mountains, were of little comfort. He placed the bone china cup on the white saucer and moved his wheelchair away from the marble coffee table. He gazed across the terrace to the shimmering waters of Lac Leman that cut a blue arc between the old Lemanic republic and Lausanne. On a clear day, Rosencrantz could see the twin towers of his old school, looming above the city suburbs. He enjoyed the castle's position on a rocky island where it commanded the approaches to the Alpine Rhone valley and the graceful city of Villeneuve.

Rosencrantz drew his heritage from the Counts of Savoy, who had kept a fearsome fleet of frigates and brigs on the lake; for him, this was home, his family seat of power. Rosencrantz glanced upward to the royal pinnacle fluttering from the medieval keep. He inhaled the scented alpine air and imbibed the sense of imperial supremacy that flowed through him as a stimulant to his damaged limbs. At times, he sensed that his shattered legs might be mysteriously repairing their torn nerves and ligaments. Rosencrantz had not given up hope that he would walk again.

Mrs. Pribble appeared in the arched doorway of the southern tower. "Phone call for you, Mr. R. On the secret line." She minced across the connecting bridge towards Rosencrantz. In her pink housekeeper's coat, pencil skirt, permed pixie bob, and cerise spectacles, Mrs. Pribble added an improbable chic to the plain uniform of the maidservant. She handed the phone to Rosencrantz.

"Thank you, Mrs. P."

"It's Mr. Kernac." Mrs. Pribble flashed a knowing smile. "Think he's got some news for you." She picked up the coffee cup and wandered along the wooden jetty and posed, with a certain elegance, one foot perched on the mooring cleat. Rosencrantz noted the seam on her retro Italian stockings.

"Rosencrantz?" Kernac's voice shook Rosencrantz from his reverie.

Rosencrantz flipped open the phone and Kernac's finely chiselled jawline appeared on the screen. He suddenly wished that Kernac was with him. "Where are you, my friend?"

"I'm on an island." Rosencrantz moved his phone to scan the curving coastline and beaches. "It's called the Mewstone. No one lives here. Just a deserted cottage with a round window." Kernac pointed the phone through the window. "Do you see that?"

Rosencrantz stared intently. "Another island."

"Yes. Burgh Island. A curious place. It has a classic Art Deco hotel. Your grandfather, Count de Boodle, visited it with all the 1930s glitterati."

Rosencrantz recalled the faded print of a photograph in the castle hallway. It showed the youthful Count dressed in a cummerbund, bow tie and shining top hat, posing with his glamorous niece, Francoise adorned in a bias-cut *crepe de chine* gown, seated on a gleaming Bechstein grand piano displaying her elegant legs and smoking a Gauloise. "I'm on an island too, my friend. I like islands. I can control what I see."

Kernac's face reappeared. "Burgh Island is just offshore. Could be useful. And you still want the boy?"

Rosencrantz shuddered and smiled grimly. "Yes, mon cher. We must get the boy." He hissed. "Where is he? And the girl."

Kernac winced and stroked his jaw, recalling Navinda's *Ushiro geri* reverse back kick that had sent him

211

tumbling down the fire escape. "The Golden Hand can have the boy, Rosencrantz. But leave the girl to me."

"As you wish, my friend. But where are they?"

"A long way away, I suspect," said Kernac. He scanned the horizon momentarily before turning back to the phone. "But we will soon know. Our friendly Hookworm will be monitoring all the Young's communications."

"Well done, mon ami. Impressive. I will not ask how you did that."

"It was surprisingly simple, Rosencrantz. The British are so naïf." Kernac's smile chased the chill from Rosencrantz's heart. "Pascal, my Breton fisherman friend will be taking me back to Cancale, and I will be dining on flat oysters and chilled Muscadet this evening. Come and join me."

"I regret not, mon cher. The French government will arrest me at the border. They are somewhat piqued at my failure to secure AlphaX for the Directorate Sécurité."

"Well, well! I will travel to Lausanne the next day. I have a plan that will amuse you." Kernac hung up. A plan that will amuse. Ha! You could always rely on Kernac. Rosencrantz gazed across the lake to the French border, feeling a new energy.

(To be continued …)

READER REVIEWS

The Upperthong Thunderbolt

A well-paced short story that grabs you from the very start. Its crisp and vibrant language will excite your mind and imagination.

Lucy Atkinson

The story is about so many important ideas, yet it had me in stitches throughout. The snooker game is hilarious, and the bit when Gilbert takes his teeth out! And Widow Wendy – what a woman! Fabulously funny.

Jon Andersen

The Angel of the North

What a beautiful, moving story, John! This might be my favourite story of yours to date. The characters truly come to life on the page, and Brenton adds a ton of comic relief. Your writing is rich, incandescent, and transported me! I love the ending as well. It's hilarious but also quite touching."

Angela Brown, editor

It is wonderfully written, I really enjoyed reading it. I loved the contrast of the ethereal with the gritty. The Angel character is very intriguing. An excellent story and characters.

Vanessa Chapman, author and book blogger

Our Man in Kampala

An eclectic – sometimes whimsical, sometimes futuristic, sometimes autobiographical and sometimes mystical – collection of short stories which offers easy and entertaining reading. One is transported, from the present to the past and the future, to some specific and some unidentified places, with imagination and feeling for characters, language and atmosphere. I particularly enjoyed *Our Man in Kampala*, in which John captures the general feel of the country, its people, its politics and its cultures, along with details of his involvement in the education system. Our Man in Uganda is an unexpected and satisfying mini travelogue to which I can return to revive my memories of a recent visit to this fascinating country.

Judy Wurr

Stargazy Pie

I loved it. A glimpse into someone else's life – but isn't that what all short stories are? I've only read it twice so far, but I got a lot more on second reading. I could see the Iroko Oji wood, I could see Izzy on Zak's mobile phone, I could see the turnip fields. I was convinced we were in New Zealand for some reason but when I went back to the text you never suggested or hinted at that. I think it must be the idea of a sacred tree and I thought cumaru sounded like a Maori word but that was only my assumption. Then I thought we were in Africa but that was simply where the block of Iroko Oji wood and the gnarled tree branch came from originally. Presumably this slightly dream-like uncertainty of location is exactly what you were trying to achieve. For your short story collection this certainly adds to the variety and *mystery* of Eva Bauer, Angel of the North and The Upper Thong Thunderbolt.

John Gardner

Julian's Wings

I loved *Julian's Wings*. The way you drip-feed the reader about John and Julian's shared history, musical and info about their relationship and its evolution. The changed perspective age brings to the world. The intimate sense of place, Ali's story, his encounters with John. The humour, the selective details betraying character and circumstance. (Aquafit, a Mamma Mia outing, Nobby's Nuts, esp. e.g., 2nd page, last paragraph lol)! Thanks for another thoroughly enjoyable read.

Nancy Owen

Picket Post

OK - wow - loved this. I chuckled at the line 'Sorry I'm black'. This is like a little morality play whose subject and message is powerful but veiled in secrecy... It gripped me and made me shudder. It's really very enjoyable.

Kip Pratt

A Game of Chess

As always, the author is a wonderful, detailed storyteller and before I knew, I was into the story. So, it really is a page turner! This is a dark and compelling tale with a beautiful love story. If you like quirky fantasy novels, this is a must-read book! I recommend it with a 5 * rating.

Kathleen Van Lierop